THE MONKEES

in

WHO'S GOT THE BUTTON?

Authorized edition based on
the popular television series

by WILLIAM JOHNSTON

Trademark of Screen Gems, Inc.

Illustrated by Richard Moore

WHITMAN PUBLISHING DIVISION
WESTERN PUBLISHING COMPANY, INC., RACINE, WISCONSIN

CONTENTS

1

The Mysterious Stranger

IN THE MIDDLE of a Monday morning, when the Monkees were at breakfast, there came a knock at the door of their pad.

"That must be opportunity," Mike said to Davy. "Why don't you get it? You have to get up to answer the door, anyway."

"What'll I tell it?" Davy asked, rising. "I've never been face to face with opportunity before."

"Invite it in for breakfast," Micky suggested. "Find out first, though, if it likes baked bananas."

Davy went to the door and opened it. A Western

Union messenger was standing outside.

"Telegram," the messenger said, offering Davy a yellow envelope.

"It does no good," Davy replied. "You can tell a gram, you can tell a gramps, you can tell a dad, you can tell a mum—but they never listen. I just don't know what's to become of this older generation."

The messenger tried again. "I have a wire for the Monkees," he said.

"Is it signed 'opportunity'?" Davy inquired, accepting the envelope.

"I don't read 'em; I just deliver 'em," the messenger replied. He extended a hand. "How about a tip?"

"A tip, eh? All right, here's a tip: Never tie your shoelaces together before starting out on a long hike," Davy advised, closing the door.

Returning to the breakfast table, Davy waved the envelope. "Telegram," he announced to the other Monkees.

"Don't open it!" Peter cried, alarmed. "Telegrams always bring bad news!"

"Right," Mike agreed. "Napoleon, as I recall, got a telegram just before he was defeated at the battle of Waterloo."

"What did it say?" Micky asked curiously.

"It said: 'Do not go to Waterloo today.' "

"What'll I do with the telegram?" Davy asked.

"Hold onto it until we're in desperate need of some bad news," Mike decided.

Davy stuffed the envelope into the sugar bowl.

The following day, Tuesday, as the Monkees were finishing breakfast, Micky grumbled, "Boy, what a dull day so far. I'd even welcome some bad news."

"We could read that telegram," Davy suggested.

"Too late," Peter said. "I had it on my corn-flakes."

"Did you by any chance read it first?" Mike asked.

"Why would I read sugar?" Peter inquired. "But I can tell you how it tasted. It tasted like it said: URGENTLY REQUEST MONKEES PARTICIPATE IN CULTURAL TOUR BELLEVUE. ALL EXPENSES PAID. IMMEDIATE REPLY REQUESTED."

"That's terrible news!" Micky sobbed. "How did it happen? And—even worse—what does it mean?"

"How did it taste like it was signed?" Mike asked Peter.

11

"Like the Government," Peter replied.

"Hmmmm . . . apparently the Government wants us to perform at Bellevue," Mike mused. "Isn't that a hospital in New York?"

"What kind of a crack is that?" Micky asked belligerently. "Is the Government trying to say our music is sick?"

"I can explain that," Peter said. "The telegram had a P. S. It tasted like it said: BELLEVUE TINY EUROPEAN KINGDOM ABOUT SIZE POSTAGE STAMP."

"That clears that up," Mike said. "As I understand it, the Government wants us to tour the tiny European kingdom of Bellevue, playing and singing, and, by the force of our winning personalities, sell the Bellevuians on the American Way of Life. Right?"

"The part about winning personalities sounds right enough," Davy replied. "But the rest of it doesn't make any sense at all."

"The question is, shall we go?" Mike asked.

"First, we'd better check the schedule and see if we can fit it in," Peter pointed out. "Anybody seen the schedule?"

"The last I saw of it, it was in the sugar bowl," Mike said.

"We better make up a new one, then," Micky said. "Let's see . . . Wednesday is the day the landlord comes for the rent, so we'll be in hiding. Thursday is the day the sheriff comes to collect for the overdue library books, so we'll be in hiding. And Fri—"

"You know, Bellevue might be a nice place to go into hiding," Davy suggested.

"Then that settles it," Mike said. "We'll get off a telegram—collect—to the Government, telling them—"

He was interrupted by a knock at the door.

"Is it Wednesday already?" Peter asked. "What happened to the rest of Tuesday?"

"That's not the landlord's knock," Davy said, heading toward the door. "He always uses both fists. That was a one-knuckle knock." He opened the door.

Crouching outside, glancing about furtively, was a small, thin, mysterious-looking stranger. He was dressed all in black: a black slouch hat pulled down over his eyes; a flowing black cape held up to cover the lower portion of his face; black silk suit; black tie; and black suede shoes.

"Is it Black Friday already?" Peter asked. "What happened to the rest of Tuesday?"

"Sh-sh-sh-sh!" the mysterious stranger warned, entering. "The walls have ears!"

He proceeded to the nearest chair, lifted the cushion, and looked under it. Satisfied, he checked the underside of the table and then inspected the lamp, peering up under the shade.

"Are you looking for anything in particular?" Micky asked. "Or just browsing?"

The mysterious stranger touched a finger to his lips. "A bug," he whispered.

"You're in the wrong room," Peter advised him. "Try the kitchen."

"He means he thinks there's a microphone planted in here," Mike explained.

Micky ran a finger through the dust on the table. "No problem," he said. "It'd never grow in this soil."

Having inspected the rest of the room thoroughly, the mysterious stranger ended the search. He smiled evilly. "All clear; we can talk now," he said. "Greetings, Monkees! I am from the Government. I am H. P. I. Smith—your interpreter. I will accompany you on your tour of the postage stamp-sized European kingdom of Bellevue, where, by the force of your winning personalities, you will sell the Bellevuians on the American Way of Life."

"H. P. I.?" Davy asked.

"Jose Pierre Ivan—I speak Spanish, French, and Russian."

"Hold it," Mike said suspiciously. "How did you get here so fast? We haven't sent our telegram of acceptance yet."

"We're trying to cut down on expenses," Smith replied. "We wanted to avoid getting a collect telegram. And, besides, we were positive you wouldn't refuse. There was one aspect of the offer that we were certain would be irresistible."

"You mean the part about culture," Davy said.

"No, the part about all expenses paid."

"That did kind of get us right here," Micky admitted, indicating his heart.

"It sure is a great honor, being asked to represent the Government in a foreign country," Peter said to Smith.

Mike still seemed somewhat suspicious. "Aren't you dressed a little oddly for an interpreter?" he asked Smith.

"Don't forget—I was a mysterious stranger before I was an interpreter," Smith replied cagily.

"Quick!" Mike challenged. "Say something in Bellevuian!"

"*E Pluribus Unum,*" Smith snapped back.

15

Mike shrugged, convinced. "For a minute, there, I thought you were a phony," he said.

"Just a doggone second," Micky said. "That's English." He got a coin from his pocket. "Look —it's right here on this American quarter."

Mike eyed Smith narrowly, his doubts revived. "Explain," he commanded.

"Elementary," Smith responded, smiling evilly once more. "English has become the official language in Bellevue. In the beginning they had no language at all—only hand signals. But they found themselves continually coming in second best in international spelling bees. Because nobody had enough hands to spell antidisestablishmentarianism. So they adopted English as their language."

"Finally, something's beginning to make sense," Mike said.

"But doesn't it raise another question?" Micky said thoughtfully. "If the Bellevuians speak English—and we speak English—why do we need an interpreter?"

"Maybe they don't speak English so good like us do," Peter suggested.

Micky shook his head. "By the evil way this guy smiles," he said, indicating Smith, "my guess is there's another answer."

"Oh . . . all right," Smith said resignedly. "I suppose you'd find out sooner or later, anyway. I'm not an interpreter. I'm a spy. I'm taking you boys with me to Bellevue to help me carry out an espionage assignment."

The Monkees peered at him, dumbfounded.

"You seem surprised," Smith said. "I don't understand why. Why else would an interpreter be dressed in a black cape, black hat, black silk suit, black tie, and black suede shoes?"

"Don't forget that you were a mysterious stranger before you were an interpreter," Peter pointed out.

"What fooled me was the black tie," Micky said. "I thought you were just coming back from a formal party."

"Now that the secret is out—how about it?" Smith asked.

"The answer is no," Mike informed him. "An unqualified, unconditional, absolute NO!"

"Good—you're keeping an open mind," Smith said. "That will make it easier for me to con you into cooperating. Let me tell you about this mission. Do you remember World War Two?"

"Not personally; but I saw the movie," Micky replied. "The part I liked best was the end,

17

where Irving, the Wonder Dog, wrapped it up single-handed. Or maybe it was single-pawed."

"That was World War One." Smith corrected him. "Pray let me continue my exposition. At the close of World War Two, with the Axis defeated, the entire colony of German scientists who had specialized in developing terrible weapons were suddenly and cruelly thrown out of work. Well, they sat around in the parks for weeks, playing chess, solving cryptograms, idling aimlessly back and forth between their benches and the water fountain. They were, in short, rapidly losing incentive."

"If this is going to be a story with a sad ending, I don't want to hear it," Micky said.

"Hold on—let me continue. It perks up. Anyway, it suddenly occurred to a highly placed but unidentified official of one of the Big Powers that the scientists' inactivity constituted a terrible waste. He sounded the alarm. 'It's later than we think!' he said. 'Before we know it, we'll be right smack-dab in the dingdong middle of World War Three, and we'll be scrambling around like a bunch of kitty cats on a hot tin roof, looking for a bunch of terrible weapons. Let's get those boys back to the drawing boards!' "

"Great story!" Davy applauded.

"Tell the part about the water fountain again," Peter urged. "That was my favorite."

"I'm not finished," Smith said. "As it eventually worked out," he continued, "the Big Powers drew straws for the scientists. Each Power got an equal number. But at the end of the drawing there was one scientist left over. No one wanted him."

A large tear rolled down Micky's cheek. "You promised it wouldn't be sad," he sobbed.

"Don't worry," Mike soothed. "I've heard this story before. The ugly duckling grows up to be a beautiful swan."

Micky beamed.

"And gets locked up in a zoo," Davy added.

Micky broke into tears again.

"As a matter of fact, that's exactly the way it happens—only without the zoo," Smith said.

Micky beamed again.

"This leftover scientist," Smith continued, "wasn't truly worthy of the name. He had never in his life invented a terrible weapon. The best he'd ever done was to invent a better mousetrap. He left it outside on the stoop one night, and it was trampled and broken when people started beating a path to his door. So, unwanted by the

19

Big Powers, he was picked up cheap by the tiny kingdom of Bellevue."

"And that's when he grew up to be a beautiful swan?" Micky guessed hopefully.

"Close." Smith smiled evilly.

"A beautiful water fountain?" conjectured Peter.

"Well. . . ."

"A beautiful water fountain in the shape of a beautiful swan?" Mike postulated.

Smith shook his head. "You'll never guess," he said. "The years passed. This honky German scientist sat tinkering away in his workshop—supported by His Highness, the king of Bellevue—coming up with one clunker after another. He invented the automobile, the airplane, the electric toothbrush—"

"Hey, that's pretty good going," Mike broke in. "Why do you call them clunkers?"

"That's another story," Smith replied. "The important thing is that finally this scientist hit the jackpot. He developed the most powerful weapon ever known to mankind."

"A beautiful water fountain in the shape of—" Peter began.

"I told you, you'd never guess," Smith interrupted. "He invented—a button!"

The Monkees stared at him, baffled.

"I don't get it," Peter said. "Where does the water come out?"

Micky looked down at the front of his shirt, panic in his eyes. *"E-e-e-e!"* he screamed. "I'm crawling with powerful weapons!"

"I can see you need a little additional filling-in," Smith said. "This button is a very special button. If punched, it would detonate every atomic bomb in the world!"

"I see," Mike nodded. "The Big Power countries have the bombs, but little ol' Bellevue has the button." He frowned thoughtfully. "Couldn't that be dangerous?"

"Worse," Smith replied. "Life has always been dangerous. But, before, it's mostly been dangerous for the other guys. Now, it's dangerous for us." He grinned evilly. "Bellevue, the only country with no atomic bombs, is the only country that's safe," he said. "Amusing, isn't it?"

"That's going to depend a lot on how careful Bellevue is with that button," Mike answered. "Suppose the button was sewed onto somebody's hip pocket and then that somebody accidentally sat down?"

"Precisely," Smith said. "That is why the button must be destroyed."

"How would you go about a thing like that?" Davy inquired. "You couldn't just hit it with a hammer."

"We'll cross that bridge when we come to it," Smith replied. "First, we must get possession of the button."

"And that's why you want us to go to Bellevue with you?" Mike asked. "To go feeling around in the dark for that button?"

"What better cover for spies?" Smith smirked evilly. "A band of innocent young troubadours and their innocent middle-aged interpreter . . . who would ever suspect?"

"I suppose it's our duty," Micky said gloomily.

"Now, wait a minute," Mike said. "Let's not jump to conclusions. How do we know what the Bellevuians intend to do with that button? For all we know, they may have nothing more serious in mind than printing 'Oh, You Kid!' on it and keeping it as a souvenir."

"Aha!" Smith giggled. "That is the 'other story' I mentioned. As the most powerful nation in the world, Bellevue is already plotting to flex her muscles!"

22

As one, the Monkees leaned forward expectantly. "Yes?" they said in unison.

"By the force of his winning personality—and The Button—" Smith explained, "King Hiram of Bellevue intends to sell the Bellevuian Way of Life to the entire world!"

"And just suppose we don't care to buy!" Micky said pugnaciously.

"*VROOOOOOM!*" Smith replied.

"He's got a pretty good selling point there," Micky admitted.

"I repeat—let's not be hasty," Mike cautioned. "What exactly is the Bellevuian Way of Life?" he asked Smith.

"It's what you might call The Good Old Days— in a word, terrible," Smith replied. "To give you an idea, the major industry in Bellevue is buggy whips."

"That *is* terrible!" Davy winced. "Anybody who would strike a buggy is no fit person to force his way of life on the rest of the world."

"Just a second—that doesn't make sense," Mike said to Smith. "Why buggy whips?"

"Because, to give you another example, the major means of transportation in Bellevue is the horse and buggy," Smith answered. "Allow me,

23

pray, to list a few more such examples for you. The principal form of entertainment in Bellevue is the Sunday band concert in King Hiram Park. The main means of communication is the pony express. And the symbol the Bellevuians worship is the chicken."

"That other stuff is understandable enough," Micky said. "But . . . the chicken? Why would anybody worship a chicken?"

"Because in Bellevue the egg is money," Smith explained. "Whereas we buy and sell by the dollar, the Bellevuians buy and sell by the egg."

"Man, they must have some awful messy vending machines," Davy said.

"They have no machines whatsoever," Smith said. "When Dr. Von Schnook, the German scientist, invented the automobile, the airplane, and the electric toothbrush, he very nearly got himself banished from the kingdom. They called him a troublemaker."

"Don't they even know about automobiles and airplanes and electric toothbrushes?" Mike asked.

"Oh, they know about them. But they refuse to accept them. The Bellevuians are dedicated to resisting progress to the very last man. They have an old saying in Bellevue that sums up their philosophy pretty neatly. It goes, 'If the chicken had intended man to have the machine, it would have given him a gas tank.' "

"Well, guys," Mike said to the other Monkees, "what do you think? Do we become spies?"

"I'm for it—if we don't have to wear black capes," Davy said. "Something has to be done about those Bellevuians. I wouldn't care to spend every Sunday at a band concert."

"And I don't think I could ever bring myself to whip a buggy," Micky said.

"Frankly, I think we're worrying about nothing," Peter said. "I still don't think they'll ever get water out of that button."

"All for one, and one for all—and that includes you," Mike said to Peter. He turned back to Smith. "We're with you," he said. "When do we leave?"

"Whenever you're ready." Smith grinned evilly. "I have a jet helicopter parked right outside. We'll parachute into Bellevue secretly."

"I thought this was supposed to be a cultural tour," Mike said. "Won't they be expecting us?"

"Of course," Smith replied. "I'm only a so-so spy. I never could keep a secret."

The Monkees collected their instruments and then, led by H. P. I. Smith, left their pad.

"This Dr. Von Schnook must be a big hero in Bellevue, the way he put the country on the map," Mike said to Smith.

Smith agreed. "He's almost as big as the chicken," he said. "In fact, he's changed his name. These days he's known as Dr. Von Durfull!"

2

The Twenty-Four Egger

AT THE CONTROLS of the jet helicopter, H. P. I.
Smith took the shortcut, and he and the Monkees
arrived over the postage stamp-sized kingdom of
Bellevue only a few hours after leaving their de-
parture point.

"That's it right down there." Smith pointed.
The Monkees looked.

"Down where?" Mike asked. "All I can see is
a little square of purple with the head of a chicken
imprinted on it."

"And the number five and an egg in one

corner," Micky added, peering out the window.

"That's it. Looks a lot like a postage stamp, doesn't it?" Smith said. "Get your parachutes. I'll circle and we'll all bail out."

"Why don't we just land?" Davy asked.

"You sure have a lot to learn about the spy business," Smith replied. "A spy always parachutes into enemy territory. Getting there is half the fun."

Smith and the Monkees strapped themselves into their parachutes. Then Smith opened the hatch and they jumped. The helicopter, pilotless, sped off into the distance.

"Isn't that a little expensive, abandoning a jet helicopter?" Mike asked as they drifted slowly toward earth.

"When you're a spy, you travel first class," Smith replied. He pointed downward. "Perfect jump," he said. "We're going to land right in the middle of the castle barnyard."

"And there's the reception committee," Davy said. "But . . . from here, they look like soldiers."

"An honor guard," Smith explained. "You'll be very big in Bellevue. The people don't see many strangers. There's a saying among experienced travelers that although Bellevue is a terrible place

to live it's an even worse place to visit."

"If it's an honor guard," Peter asked, "why do the soldiers have their bayonets pointing up?"

"They want to make sure you stick around," Smith explained.

As Smith and the Monkees neared the ground, the soldiers moved back, forming a circle. A moment later, Smith and the Monkees dropped into the center of it.

The commander of the soldiers stepped forward. "In the name of King Hiram, I welcome you to Bellevue," he announced. He signaled to one of his men. "Frisk 'em," he ordered.

"There's no need for that," Smith said to the commander. "I checked them out, and they don't have one thing worth stealing."

The commander clicked his heels and saluted.

"Man, you sure have pull around here," Davy said to Smith.

"I give them a lot of my spying business," Smith replied. "They appreciate it." He addressed the commander again. "Take us to King Hiram," he said. "He's expecting us."

Once more the commander clicked his heels and saluted. Then he and his men marched the Monkees and Smith toward the rear door of the castle. The barnyard animals—geese, cows, horses, pigs, sheep—honked, mooed, neighed, oinked, and baaed as they passed.

"King Hiram must not be very well-off," Mike commented. "No chickens."

Smith winced. "Chickens in a dirty old barnyard?" he said. "The chickens have the top floor of the castle. That floor offers the best view of the countryside. Nothing is too good for the chicken."

"They ought to like me here in Bellevue, then," Peter said. "I've always been a little chicken myself."

Lowering his voice, Mike spoke to Micky, who was walking next to him. "Don't you think it's a little odd how that commander took orders from Smith?" he asked.

"Smith explained that, he gives them the business," Micky replied.

"Think about it," Mike said. "If he spies on them, why would they give him so much respect?"

"Simple," Micky answered. "For the same reason they keep chickens on the top floor of the castle—we're in a loony bin!"

Mike shook his head. "That explains a lot, but not everything. I think there's something about this chicken mission that Smith hasn't told us."

They entered the castle, proceeded along a corridor, then reached another doorway. The commander ushered them into a room that looked a great deal like an old-time farm kitchen. There was a huge cast-iron stove, into which a gray-haired old lady, wearing a faded gingham dress, was pitching corncobs. In one corner was a washtub and washboard. Seated at the large kitchen table was a big, ruddy-faced fellow. He had chin whiskers and was dressed in overalls and boots. Around his neck was a red bandanna, and perched sideways on his head was a gold crown.

"This is the throne room," Smith said to the Monkees. "And, as you've probably guessed, this is King Hiram." He then addressed the king. "Here they are, Your Highness—the Monkees," he said.

"Howdy, boys." The king smiled amiably. He hooked a thumb toward the gray-haired old lady. "That there's Maw," he said. Then, turning toward his mother, he said, "Better whistle up Ellie Jo, Maw. She'd sour the honey pot if she found out we let the company get away 'fore she seen 'em."

Maw put two fingers between her teeth and shattered the quiet with a shrill whistle.

"That'll bring her." The king chuckled. He faced the Monkees again. "Pull up a chair and squat," he said. "I reckon we can get crackin' on this welcomin' ceremony. That's one of my chores, as king. I got to glad-hand every Tom, Dick, and Harry that lights in town. First time I ever laid out the red carpet for a clutch of Monkees, though." He sighed woefully. "Kingin' ain't what it used to be."

"Things are bound to pick up once you take over the world, son," his mother said comfortingly.

"Yep!" King Hiram nodded. "There'll be some changes made, all right."

"What sort of changes?" Davy asked.

"I'll undo all the changes that've been made," the king replied.

"That'll be a change," Davy acknowledged.

At that moment a young lady about the age of the Monkees entered the throne room. She was beautiful. Her blond hair was in pigtails and she was wearing a brightly colored calico dress.

"You whistle, Gran'maw?" she asked.

"I wasn't tootin' on the organ," the queen mother replied.

The king introduced the young lady to the Monkees. She was Ellie Jo, his daughter. She blushed as the introductions were made.

"Maw, rustle up some eggnogs," the king

ordered. "The boys must be dry after that long trip."

"It wasn't very long—we took the shortcut," Mike said.

"Need the eggnogs for the ceremony, anyways," King Hiram said. "I got to toast you boys and your country to make the welcomin' official. We don't hold back none when we get company. Only the best."

"Has there been any publicity about our cultural tour yet?" Mike asked the king. "A few stories in the newspapers always help to draw a crowd."

The king frowned. "Ain't got no newspapers," he said.

"Ain't got no news," Ellie Jo explained. "Don't nothin' happen in Bellevue." She smiled affectionately at her father. "Paw don't let it," she said.

"Ellie Jo's right," King Hiram said. "Last time anything like news happened in Bellevue was in 1764 when old Dan Barnthistle's prize hen laid an egg with a double yolk."

"What about The Button?" Micky asked. "Isn't that news?"

"Yep, I reckon that's right," the king replied. "But having one little speck of news ain't no cause to start up a whole newspaper. Say we printed the story about The Button. What would we do the next day? We'd be stuck with a newspaper and nothin' to put in it. Leave well enough alone— that's my motto."

The queen mother handed around the glasses of eggnog.

"Well, here's to you boys," the king said, raising his glass, beginning the toast. "And, while we're about it, here's to that funny-lookin' country you come from, too."

"What's so funny-looking about the United States?" Peter asked.

"It ain't square," King Hiram replied. "It's got all them bulges stickin' out. The right shape for a country is like a postage stamp. Any doggone fool knows that."

"Paw knows it," Ellie Jo said sweetly.

King Hiram raised his glass again. "We-all in Bellevue want you boys to know it sure is an honor to have you as our guests," he continued. "It sure is neighborly of you, bringin' your high-toned culture over here to share with us plain folk. 'Course, there's some that might say, 'Who needs it?' But nobody'll hear 'em. 'Cause they don't get invited to official ceremonies like this."

35

"That's very nice of you to say that—I think," Mike replied. "And, speaking for all of us—"

"I ain't finished," the king interrupted.

"Oh."

"Next, we drink up," King Hiram said.

They all sipped from their glasses.

"How's them eggnogs?" the queen mother asked.

"A little rich," Micky replied.

"Should be, them's five-egg eggnogs," she said.

"Well, thank the chicken, that's finished," the king said. He turned to Smith. "You can call them soldiers in and tell them they can throw these spies in the dungeon now," he said. "Myself, I'm due for a little snooze. This hospitality wears me out. It ain't natural."

"The dungeon?" all the Monkees shouted in unison.

"Surely you don't think we let spies run around loose," Smith said.

"What do you mean, 'we'?" Micky asked. "You're supposed to be on our side."

"Oh—did I forget to mention that?" Smith replied. "Actually, I only pretend to be a spy for the United States. I'm really a spy for Bellevue."

"Then why did you bring us over here to help you find The Button?" Davy inquired.

"Orders," Smith answered. "The U.S. doesn't know I'm a spy for Bellevue. It thinks I'm a spy for the U.S. So, as a spy for the U.S., I was ordered to get you to help me find The Button and destroy it. All along, however, I've really been working for Bellevue."

"Don't you sometimes get a little confused?" Peter asked.

"Only on my days off, when I do a little free-lance spying for Russia," Smith replied.

"What I don't understand is what good this is going to do anybody," Davy said.

"What bad it's going to do anybody, you mean," Smith said. "And the answer to that is quite simple. I'll keep sending reports back to Washington, telling them we're hot on the trail of The Button. In the meantime, The Button will be completely safe. Because you will be locked up in a cell in the dungeon."

"I like it," Micky said. "I think it'll work."

King Hiram yawned. "You gonna stand around jawin'," he said crossly to Smith, "or are you gonna get them soldier fellas?"

"Coming up, Your Highness," Smith replied, moving toward the door.

"It sure has been a pleasure meetin' you boys,"

37

Ellie Jo said to the Monkees, blushing again. "If you ever break out of that dungeon, you be sure and call again—hear?"

"What's a nice princess like you doing in a kingdom like this?" Davy asked. "With your looks and that blush, you could be on color television."

Princess Ellie Jo had no opportunity to reply. For at that moment the soldiers entered the throne room and hustled the Monkees out. They took them down a long corridor and then down a long flight of stone steps. Finally they reached the dungeon. A guard was standing sentry duty at a row of cells.

"Four prisoners for you, compliments of King Hiram," the commander of the soldiers announced to the guard.

"Strange-lookin' boys, ain't they?" the guard, a tall, lanky youth, replied. "With all that hair, you can tell they're criminals, all right. I always say, show me a fella with long hair and I'll show you a—" He interrupted himself, looked thoughtful for a moment, and then asked, "What's the charge?"

"Spying," the commander replied.

"—and I'll show you a dirty, doggone, lily-livered spy," the guard concluded. He opened a cell door and motioned to the Monkees. "Inside, you culprits."

When the Monkees had been securely locked behind bars, the soldiers departed and the guard began marching back and forth, back and forth, in front of the cells.

"I don't want to be an alarmist," Mike said to the other Monkees, "but I'm beginning to think we should never have left home."

"What are you worried about?" Peter asked, looking at his watch. "The cake will be along any minute now."

"That soon?" Davy asked, surprised. "What time is it?"

"Five minutes till cake," Peter replied.

"Why am I always the last to know!" Micky complained. "What cake?"

"The cake with the saw in it," Davy explained. "When somebody is put in a cell, somebody else always shows up about five minutes later with a cake with a saw in it."

"We better not depend on that," Mike decided. "Our only chance, as I see it, is to trick the guard. Micky, you start groaning. Pretend that you're sick. Then, when the guard comes in to find out what's wrong, we'll jump him. Okay? Now!"

Micky stretched out on one of the cots. "Oh! My tum-tum!" he groaned.

"Where does it hurt?" Peter asked sympathetically.

"Just a little bit north of North Carolina," Micky replied. He clutched his head. "Oh! My poor tum-tum! Tell me the truth, Doctor! I can take it!"

"I think you have a misplaced tum-tum," Peter said.

The guard stopped at the cell door. "What's going on in there?" he demanded.

"My friend is sick!" Mike said. "Do something!"

"Sick, eh?" the guard replied coldly. "I'm not surprised. That long hair will do it every time."

"He needs help!" Mike pleaded.

"I can't help him," the guard said. "I'm not a doctor."

"Then get a doctor!"

The guard shook his head. "Not a chance," he said. "Doctors don't make cell calls these days." He resumed marching.

Micky sat up. "It's a miracle—I'm cured!" he cried joyfully.

"And they told your tum-tum it would never walk again," Davy said with a cynical smile. "It just goes to prove: Where there's—"

"Howdy, boys," a feminine voice interrupted.

Turning, the Monkees found Princess Ellie Jo outside the cell door. She was carrying a thickly iced angel food cake.

"Am I late?" she asked.

"Nope—right on time," Peter replied, glancing at his watch.

"Guard!" Princess Ellie Jo called. "Let me into the cell, please. I'm gonna interrogate these terrible ol' spies."

"Do you think it's safe, Princess?" the guard asked worriedly, unlocking the cell door. "I understand that long hair is catching."

"I guess it wouldn't hurt me none, me bein' a girl," she replied. "But if it troubles you, why don't you go off somewheres where you can't see what's goin' on?"

"Gee, thanks. You're a princess, Princess," the guard said. And after letting Ellie Jo into the cell and locking the door again, he moved on down the corridor out of sight.

"I'll bet you've got something for us in that cake," Micky said to the princess, grinning.

"Sure enough," she answered, blushing. "I reckon I just plumb couldn't stand it, havin' you boys locked up like a bunch of animals. What's in this cake'll get you out—no maybes about that."

"Just a minute," Mike said suspiciously. "Why are you doing this? Don't you realize that if we get out of here we'll start looking for The Button? And that when we find it we'll destroy it?"

"But that's why, punkins," Princess Ellie Jo replied. "I *want* you to find that button and destroy it. I declare I haven't had a minute's happiness since that ol' button got itself invented. I got to think about my future."

"Your future?" Mike said, puzzled. "Your father will be king of the world. And that will make you princess of the world. What's so terrible about that, futurewise?"

"It'd just ruin my whole life, that's all," Princess Ellie Jo said sorrowfully. "You know what Daddy's got in mind? He's gonna turn the whole world into one big ol' Bellevue. Everybody everywhere's not gonna have the same things we ain't got here. They ain't gonna have automobiles, and they ain't gonna have airplanes, and they ain't gonna have electric toothbrushes—they just ain't gonna have nothin'. I'll tell you, havin' nothin' is just gonna be common as dirt. Now, that means somethin'. It ain't everybody that ain't got nothin'. But

when everybody ain't got nothin'—who wants it?"

The Monkees looked at each other blankly.

"You see," Princess Ellie Jo continued, "as it is, bein' a princess, naturally, I got more nothin' than anybody. It's kind of a privilege of rank— you know? And that sets me apart. I mean, I'm somebody. But when everybody in the whole world has nothin'. . . . Well, it's gonna take the status right out of it."

"I think I see what she means," Mike said. "She means—"

"Don't start that again!" Davy broke in. "We all see what she means."

"So I brought you this cake," Princess Ellie Jo said. "And, just to make it even easier, I'm gonna tell you where you can find that horrible ol' Dr. Von Durfull and his silly ol' button. He's up in the tower."

"You mean he's a prisoner, too?" Peter asked.

"Land sakes, no, sugar," Ellie Jo replied. "He's up there toilin'. He— Just a minute," she said. She closed her eyes tightly and blushed. "If I don't do that blush ever' once in a while, I get out of practice," she explained. "Now, then, what was I sayin'?"

"Dr. Von Durfull. . . ."

"He's up there in the tower hidin' away—so none of you spy fellas'll find him," the princess continued. "But he's also studyin' The Button. You see, he don't recollect how he put it together, and, bein' a scientist, he's curious. They're all like that—nosy, nosy, nosy."

"Princess, your troubles are over," Micky said. "The instant we get out of this cell we'll rush up to the tower and destroy that button."

"I just knew I could depend on you." The princess blushed.

"Uh . . . one thing . . . which way to the tower?" Micky asked.

"Up, dumplin'."

"It gets easier all the time," Micky replied. "Now, if you'll just hand over the cake. . . ."

"I'll give it to this one," Ellie Jo said, putting the cake in Mike's hands. "Anybody who don't know that a tower is up shouldn't be trusted with anything valuable. That cake is a dozen-egger."

"Wow!" Peter said, inspecting the cake from all angles. "What's the icing worth?"

"Another dozen eggs in that icin'," Ellie Jo replied. "In fact, my whole month's allowance is tied up in that cake, so don't you fail me."

"Don't worry—it's like money in the bank,"

45

Davy promised. "We'll make sure that you never have to worry about your nothing again."

Princess Ellie Jo summoned the guard. He opened the cell door and let her out. Then, as she departed, he locked it again.

"Say, that's a jim-dandy cake," the guard said, peering into the cell. "Looks like about a twenty-four egger—counting the icing."

"Hadn't you better get back to your marching?" Mike asked.

The guard ignored the question. "Not much I wouldn't do for a twenty-four egger," he said hungrily.

"Hup! One, two, three! March!" Micky commanded.

The guard sighed sadly and then reluctantly resumed walking his post.

The instant he was out of sight, the Monkees dived at the cake. They tore it piece from piece. Icing splattered.

"No saw!" Micky groaned.

"It must be here somewhere!" Davy insisted. "No girl who blushes like that could be a double-crosser."

"Tear it into smaller pieces," Mike said. "Maybe it's a miniature saw."

Frantic, they ripped the pieces into pieces. But the result was the same.

"No saw," Micky groaned again.

"I can't believe it," Davy said. "So much depended on this. Why did the princess bring us this cake if it doesn't have a saw in it?"

The guard stopped at the cell door again. "Cracky! That sure is a mess in there," he said. "Too bad, too. With a twenty-four egger like that, you could have bribed me and escaped and got hold of The Button and made Bellevue safe for nothing again. But . . . it's not worth much now."

"I guess that explains why she brought us the cake," Mike said to Davy.

Davy looked gloomily at the cake and icing clinging to his fingers; then he shrugged. "Easy come . . . easy go," he said.

3

A Wild-Goose Chase

LOOK AT THIS cell!" Micky complained to the guard. "It's strewn with cake and plastered with icing from side to side and top to bottom. We demand new quarters."

"It sure is strewn, all right—whatever that means," the guard admitted. "Looks doggone near good enough to eat. Cracky! I sure wish you was out here and I was in there!"

Micky sidled up to the bars. "Maybe that could be arranged," he said, lowering his voice. "Try bribing us."

The guard shook his head. "Couldn't afford it," he replied. "Even used, that cake's still a twenty-four egger."

"Scoff, scoff," Micky scoffed. "You're a Bellevuian, so I'll bet you've got plenty of nothin' stashed away. Try a little of that."

Again the guard shook his head. "That's put away for my retirement," he said. "Tell you what I'll do, though. I'll clean up that cell for you."

"I guess that's better than nothing," Micky replied, resigned.

"Just wait'll I get my bib," the guard said, moving away.

Micky motioned to the other Monkees and they huddled around him in conference.

"This is our chance," he whispered. "When the guard enters the cell, we'll jump him."

"That's not fair," Peter said. "There are four of us and one of him."

"I know." Micky nodded. "But where will we get anybody else to help us?"

At that moment the guard reappeared. He was wearing a bib and carrying a pistol. Excited, he opened the door and stepped into the cell. Then, holding the gun on the Monkees, he sat down on a cot, picked up a chunk of cake with his free

49

hand, and began devouring it greedily.

"I understand about us jumping him, but who's going to jump his friend?" Mike asked Micky, indicating the pistol.

"This calls for new strategy," Micky replied. "Anybody got any ideas?"

"Let's give up," Peter suggested.

"Brilliant!" Davy said.

"The motion has been made and seconded that we give up," Micky said. "How do we vote?"

"Owwwww!" the guard suddenly cried, leaping up.

"That's one *owwwww!* in favor," Micky said. "How about the rest of you?"

The guard was hopping around the cell, pressing his hands to his cheeks. "My cavity!" he wailed. *"Owwwwww!"* Doubled over by pain, he rushed toward the open door. But under such conditions his aim was not the best. He missed the opening and butted into the bars—and then crumpled up and dropped to the floor, unconscious.

The Monkees gathered around him.

"This is a great moment in history," Mike said solemnly. "This man has discovered what human beings have sought for centuries—an alternative to going to the dentist."

"But it's the easy way out. It'll never catch on," Davy said.

Micky motioned toward the open doorway. "Anybody for the tower?" he asked.

With Micky in the lead, the Monkees slipped out of the cell. They crept quietly up the stairway to the main floor, then halted.

"The question now is, where's the elevator?" Micky said.

"Castles don't have elevators," Mike said. "You have to take the secret passageway. Let's find the library. The secret passageway is always behind the bookshelves."

"The question now is, where's the library?" Micky said.

"Straight down this corridor, take a turn to the left, then another turn to the left, then a third turn to the left," H. P. I. Smith replied.

The Monkees turned and found the secret agent standing at the end of the line.

"That would bring us right back here where we are," Peter pointed out.

"Exactly." Smith smiled evilly. He pointed to a door across the corridor. "That's it."

"Thanks for your help," Mike said. "If there's ever anything we can do for you, just name it."

51

"Freddie," Smith said.

"Freddie?"

"That's my name for 'surrender,'" Smith answered.

"Well, we'd be glad to," Mike began. "But—"

"Guards!" Smith bellowed.

Soldiers suddenly appeared at both ends of the corridor.

"Seize them!" Smith shouted.

Micky counted the guards. "Sorry," he said to Smith. "We'd like to oblige, but there are just too many of them."

The guards came racing along the corridor toward them from both directions.

"Into the library!" Mike said, heading for the door that Smith had pointed out.

Micky, Peter, and Davy hurried after him.

"I don't think we ought to do this," Peter said worriedly. "We already owe money on overdue books back home. We could get in trouble."

"We'll just browse," Davy said.

"I can't do that," Peter fretted. "When I find an interesting book, I just have to read it."

"Sick-sick-sick!" Mickey said disgustedly.

Mike yanked open the door to the library. The Monkees crowded through the opening. Then

Mike quickly shut the door and locked it.

"There we are," Mike said smugly, "trapped!"

Outside, fists began pounding on the door.

"Trapped—but not for long," Davy said. "Rescue is on the way. I give that door about five minutes."

"Find the secret passageway," Mike said.

The Monkees began racing about the room, pressing on walls, looking for cracks, opening desk drawers, moving furniture, and bumping into each other. Meanwhile the pounding continued.

"Two minutes till disaster," Peter reported, looking at his watch.

"Go read a book!" Mike snapped.

Peter walked to the shelves and began perusing the titles. "This looks interesting," he said. *"How to Build Your Own Printing Press and Make Money on Wall Street—or Any Other Street, For That Matter."*

There was a splintering sound. A panel in the door had been knocked out. A hand reached through and groped for the lock.

"It's disaster time!" Micky sang out.

Peter took the book from the shelf. And, as he did, the whole shelf swung back, revealing a secret passageway.

"Cut that out!" Peter scolded. "Now I don't know where this book goes!"

The hand found the door lock, unlatched it, and then turned the knob. The door burst open. Smith and the soldiers crowded into the room.

"Seize them!" Smith shouted.

"We'll make a deal," Mike replied. "If you can get them to line up, faces to the wall and hands over their heads, we'll make a try at it. But I still say there're too many of them."

The guards rushed at the Monkees.

The Monkees rushed at the secret passageway.

The Monkees won. Plunging into darkness, they found themselves dashing blindly up a stairway. Behind them they could hear the soldiers in hot pursuit.

Micky, who was in the lead, called back. "I see a crack of light up ahead!"

"How far ahead?" Davy asked.

There was a sudden crash. Micky had plowed into a door and kept right on going. "About a sixteenth of an inch," he replied, inspecting the hole he had made.

Mike, Davy, and Peter followed him through the opening.

"Where are we?" Peter asked.

"Now, this is just a wild guess," Micky replied. "But, offhand, I'd say we were in the private bed-chamber of King Hiram of Bellevue." He pointed toward the far side of the room, where King Hiram, seated on the edge of a canopied bed and wearing a red nightshirt, was staring at them grumpily. "Exhibit A," Micky said.

"You boys know you're trespassin'?" King Hiram complained. "Right after my snooze, I'm gonna pass a law against that!"

"Seize them!" a voice shouted from the secret passageway.

The Monkees raced across the room, whipped open the door, and darted out into the corridor.

Behind them, they heard King Hiram call out, "They went thataway!"

With Peter in the lead this time, the Monkees galloped down the corridor. They reached a stairway. Peter raced downward, with Micky, Mike, and Davy at his heels.

"Why didn't we go up?" Mike asked. "That's the way to the tower."

"It's not allowed," Peter panted. "This is a down staircase, and it's against the rules to go up a down staircase. I read that in a book."

"Take a note," Mike said to Davy. "No more

55

books for Peter. He can't handle them."

"Halt—in the name of the king!" a familiar voice cried from behind.

Davy looked back. The king, in his red night-shirt, was now leading the chase.

"All is lost!" Davy said. "With three feet, the king will be able to outrun us easily."

Mike glanced back. "What three feet?"

"Doesn't every ruler have three feet?" Davy asked.

"That's a yardstick," Mike replied. "A ruler is only twelve inches."

Once more, Davy looked back. "He certainly is tall for that size," he said.

They reached the main floor. Peter led them across the entranceway and out the door. Then he headed toward the rear of the castle.

"I suppose you have some plan in mind," Micky said to Peter.

"I'm going to circle around and come up behind them and let them take the lead," Peter replied. "They know the castle better than we do."

A moment later, the Monkees reached the barnyard—and came upon Princess Ellie Jo, who was feeding the geese.

"Quick—where can we hide?" Peter said.

Ellie Jo looked at the Monkees disapprovingly. "Hide?" she said. "If you need a place to hide, then you must be being chased. And if you're being chased, you must be the losers. It just wouldn't be seemly for a princess to get herself mixed up with a bunch of losers," she said.

The king, Smith, and the soldiers came racing around the corner of the castle.

"Over here, Paw!" Ellie Jo called out. "I found 'em for you!"

The Monkees took off again, running toward the rear door of the castle.

"Take another note," Mike said to Davy. "Never trust a princess who blushes."

As the Monkees reached the rear door of the castle, they looked back and saw that they were now being pursued by Ellie Jo, the king, Smith, and the soldiers.

"Next, it'll be the geese," Davy said.

They heard a loud honk behind them. Piling through the doorway, the Monkees looked back once more. The geese had joined the chase.

"One more note," Mike said to Davy. "From now on, do as the Bellevuians do: Leave well enough alone."

Inside the castle, the Monkees scampered down

the corridor. They came to a fork.

"This way!" Mike said, turning left.

"No, this way!" Micky said, turning right.

Davy followed Mike. Peter followed Micky.

Seconds later, the king, the princess, Smith, the guards, and the geese reached the fork.

"They went this way," the king said, turning left.

"No—I saw them go this way," Smith said, turning right.

The princess and the guards followed the king. The geese followed Smith.

Ahead, Mike and Davy came to a corner and turned right. In another part of the castle, Micky and Peter reached a corner and turned left.

The king, the princess, and the guards, following Mike and Davy, lost sight of them temporarily and turned left instead of right. When Smith and the geese reached the corner that Micky and Peter had just turned, Smith took a left and the geese took a right.

Reaching another corner, Mike and Davy found the king, the princess, and the guards racing toward them from the opposite direction.

"This way!" Mike said.

"That way!" Davy argued.

Mike ran his way and Davy ran his way. A moment later, Mike turned another corner and found himself racing along in the middle of the geese. Davy, meanwhile, had turned a different corner and discovered himself running along behind Smith.

Not far away, the king and the princess and the guards turned a corner and collided head-on with Micky and Peter. There was a wild scramble.

Micky got to his feet first and ran off in one direction. The king, the next up, set out in pursuit of him. Peter, seeing what had happened, fled in the opposite direction. And the guards, the next to last to rise, galloped after Peter.

Princess Ellie Jo did not bother to get up. She calculated how the mix-up would end, and elected to let the others come to her. And not long after, the king, Smith, the guards, the geese, and the Monkees all appeared at the same time from around different corners and met. There was a grand pile-up. Ellie Jo, unfortunately, found herself at the bottom of it.

Micky leaped up from the spaghetti of arms and legs and blew shrilly on a referee's whistle.

"Awright! Awright!" he roared. "What a bunch of bumblers! How do you think this looks from the grandstand? On your feet! Let's run through it once more, and let's get it right this time!"

Dazed, the others dragged themselves to their feet.

"Awright now, you, boy!" Micky said to the king, pointing him down the corridor. "You're my lead-off man. I want you to go straight ahead, then left, then right, then left-right, then right-left-right. Got that? Okay, you're on your own, boy. Go!"

Groggy, the king stumbled forward and disappeared down the corridor.

"Follow that king!" Micky snapped at Smith. "Let's get a little pepper into it! Hike—one, two, three! Go!"

Smith staggered off in the direction in which the king had gone.

"Awright, geese, are you going to stand around like a bunch of geese?" Micky snarled.

Honking noisily, the geese followed Smith.

"And you—" Micky said to the princess.

"You ain't gonna send me off with them losers, are you, dumplin'?" Ellie Jo asked. "Now? When you need me? When I'm the only one around who can tell you how to get to the tower?"

"Awright, you're sidelined, sister!" Micky

barked. He turned to the guards. "You men in the backfield, I want you to get out there and find that line. Then I want you to hit it!" he ordered. "Let's go now!" he said, moving among the guards and patting them encouragingly on the back. "Let's win this one for the old school!"

Weaving from side to side, the guards stumbled off.

Micky smiled after them proudly. "There goes the best bunch of boys eggs can buy," he said. He turned back to Princess Ellie Jo. "Which way to the tower?" he asked urgently.

She pointed to a sign that, in turn, pointed to a stairway. The sign said: TO THE TOWER. "Just follow your eyes," she said.

The Monkees peered dimly at the sign.

"No U-Turn?" Davy asked, trying to shake off the daze.

"Free Lunch?" Peter blinked.

"Made in Texas by Texans?" Mike asked doubtfully.

Micky clapped his hands sharply. "Awright, you boys on the second team!" he snapped. "Let's show 'em what we're made of! On your toes! Follow me! Up that U-Turn, grab that Free Lunch, and Remember the Alamo! Yo!"

Micky bounded up the steps, and Mike, Peter, and Davy went struggling after him. They proceeded up step after step after step after step. Finally they reached a closed door. Micky tried to turn the knob, but the door was locked.

"We'll have to break it down," he said.

"Hold it—I'm not ready," Peter said.

"What's the problem?"

"I forgot the Alamo," Peter answered.

"Awright, you stand back," Micky said. "The three of us will handle it. Ready? One, two—"

The door opened. A small man dressed in a baggy suit looked out at the Monkees. He was bald and wrinkle-faced, and his rimless spectacles were perched at the tip of his long nose.

"Vot's dot noise?" the man asked irritably.

"That was me," Peter replied. "I'm trying to remember the Alamo."

"Who you?" The man glared at them.

Peter pointed to Micky. "I'm his assistant," he answered.

"Dr. Von Durfull, I presume." Micky smiled. "We're the official button inspectors. We understand that you have a button in there that hasn't been inspected."

"Can't destroy the whole world with an uninspected button, you know," Mike said. "That could get you in a peck of trouble."

"Nobody told me about no button inspection," Dr. Von Durfull grumbled.

"It's a surprise inspection," Davy explained. "If you'd been told about it, it wouldn't be a surprise, would it? See how it all works out?"

"Ya, dot makes sense." Dr. Von Durfull nodded. "Okay," he said, opening the door wider to let the Monkees pass, "but make it quick. I never had a button inspected before. It don't take long, does it?"

"How would we know?" Micky replied, leading the way into the room. "We've never inspected a button before."

Dr. Von Durfull closed the door, then joined them.

"Just a minute," Micky said. He reopened the door. "Just in case there's a regulation against inspecting a button in a closed room, or in case somebody might want to make a fast getaway," he explained to the scientist. "Now," he said, "let's see that button."

Dr. Von Durfull pointed to a small, black object that was resting on a small, square, white object. "The one on top is The Button," he said.

"The one on bottom is the table."

Micky bent over the button, inspecting it closely. "Mmmmmmm . . . button-like, isn't it?"

"Button-shaped, too." Dr. Von Durfull nodded. "I got dot part down perfect. What beats me is what's inside the button. I just kept puttin' stuff in, a little dis, a little dot, until all of a sudden I found myself with The Button."

"I think this calls for a conference," Micky said. He motioned to Davy, Mike, and Peter. They joined him in a corner of the room.

"Why do we need a conference?" Davy asked. "There it is. Why don't we just grab it and run?"

"The problem is, how are we going to destroy it?" Micky replied. "One wrong move and we could blow up the entire world."

"Let Washington worry about that," Mike suggested.

"See? That's why we needed a conference," Micky said. "So, after putting our heads together, we could come to an intelligent, logical conclusion. Now—let's grab it and run!"

The Monkees broke from the huddle and dived for the table. They got the table. But The Button eluded them. It dropped to the floor and rolled toward the open doorway.

"Stop, you inspectors!" Von Durfull shouted. "But's my dotton!"

"I think you mean 'dot's my button,' " Mike corrected him.

"Oh . . . ya," Von Durfull agreed. "I don't know the language so good."

"Get it!" Davy cried woefully. "It's rolling down the steps!"

The Monkees dashed through the doorway and raced down the stairs in pursuit of The Button.

Von Durfull watched them as they chased after it. He sighed. "Ah, vell . . . easy come, easy go." He shrugged.

Step by step, The Button bounced downward. Behind it, also step by step, the Monkees tumbled over one another.

Finally, The Button bounced off the bottom step and then rolled out into the middle of the corridor.

The Monkees closed in on it.

"Easy now! Don't jar it!" Micky warned. "It can't get away."

Step by step, they moved closer.

But as they neared the bottom of the stairs, they heard a sudden thundering sound.

"I think it's going to rain," Peter said.

"That's the thunder of hoofbeats!" Davy said.

He peeked around the corner of the stairway. "Back!" he cried, alarmed, shoving the others out of the way.

As the Monkees watched, appalled, King Hiram went galloping past, narrowly missing The Button.

"Whew! Close!" Micky said, relieved.

"Back!" Davy cried again.

Once more a thundering was heard. Then H. P. I. Smith went charging past—barely missing The Button.

"Now?" Mike asked.

"Back!" Davy cried once more.

The guards went galloping past—narrowly missing The Button.

"That's the king and Smith and the guards—and that's all," Mike said. "Can we get The Button now?"

"Back!" Davy shouted again.

From the corridor came a honking sound. Then the geese went thundering past.

"They missed The Button!" Davy cried happily.

Mike peeked around the corner. "Not yet. One more to go," he reported.

The others joined him in peeking around the corner. A solitary goose was approaching. Its wings were dragging, its tail was drooping.

"Awright, if you can't keep up the pace—off the team!" Micky barked.

The goose honked dismally. Then, perhaps in retaliation for being kicked off the team, it struck back. It picked up The Button in its bill, raised its long neck, gulped, and swallowed.

"I'll make you a deal," Micky said. "Give us back The Button, and not only will I put you back on the team, but you can also be the coach and the grandstand."

The goose honked derisively.

"Get 'im!" Micky shouted.

The Monkees dived for the goose. Terrified, the goose flapped wildly out of their grasp and flew out of a window.

"Gone goose!" Micky sobbed.

4

To the Rack—and Back

THE MONKEES RUSHED to the window. They saw the goose land in the barnyard.

"We can still get The Button back," Mike said. "Our goose is the only goose down there. All the others are still chasing the king and the guards."

"But even if we catch him," Davy said, "how will we get The Button? He swallowed it!"

"There's one chance," Micky replied. "You being the smallest, you'll have to go in after it."

The Monkees dashed down the corridor, and then, reaching a stairway, they fell down the steps to the ground floor. They ended up in a pile at the bottom.

"Seize them!" a voice shouted.

Looking up, they saw King Hiram, Smith, the guards, and the geese at the top of the steps.

The Monkees scrambled to their feet and raced toward the door. King Hiram, Smith, the guards, and the geese thundered down the stairs in pursuit.

"We've got to get that goose before those geese get to that goose," Micky said frantically. "If our goose gets mixed up with those other geese, we'll have a gone goose again."

The Monkees dashed out the back door of the castle and into the barnyard. They spotted the goose. Again, they dived at it. And again, honking wildly, the goose flapped into the air.

Once more, the Monkees ended up in a pile.

King Hiram, Smith, the guards, and the other geese arrived.

"Seize them!" King Hiram shouted to the guards.

At that moment, the goose that had swallowed The Button landed in the midst of the other geese.

The Monkees, meanwhile, had been seized by the guards.

"Dog take it!" King Hiram said. "You boys sure run a fella a merry chase. I ain't had so much exercise since that day the live frog jumped up my pants leg."

"Tell us about it," Davy said, interested.

"Well, I was down at the creek—"

"Your Highness," Smith interrupted, "hadn't we better get these spies back to the dungeon? While they're free, The Button isn't safe."

The king glared at him. "How come, Smith, every time I start to tell that story about the live frog you think of somethin' else I ought to be doin'?"

"Your Highness, I was only—" He broke in on himself and pointed toward the back door of the castle. "Here comes Dr. Von Durfull," he said. "I hope someone is guarding The Button."

"It's in a very safe place," Davy assured him, glancing toward the flock of geese.

"You got them!" Dr. Von Durfull said happily. He held out a hand. "Who's got The Button?" he asked.

"Who's got The Button?" King Hiram inquired, puzzled. "You got The Button."

Dr. Von Durfull shook his head. "They got The Button," he said. "I had The Button, but they took it from me. So they must have The Button. If they ain't got The Button, then who has got The Button?"

"Ask the geese," Mike suggested.

Dr. Von Durfull turned to the geese. "You got The Button?" he asked.

"Dagnabit! Hold on!" the king said. "Are you tellin' me these boys took that button from you? How'd that happen?"

Dr. Von Durfull explained to the king that the Monkees had pretended to be button inspectors.

"Then they still got it!" King Hiram decided. "Frisk 'em!" he ordered.

The guards began searching the Monkees.

"I knew I should've had them frisked when they first got here," King Hiram complained to Smith. "Why'd you stop me? If we'd frisked 'em then, we wouldn't be havin' to do it now—we'd have The Button."

"That was before they stole The Button, Your Highness," Smith pointed out.

The king nodded resignedly. "I knew you'd figure out some excuse."

"They don't have The Button, Your Highness," the head guard reported.

"Try frisking the geese," Peter suggested.

72

"Leave my geese out of it!" the king roared. "Them's royal geese! And royal is loyal! If them geese had that button, they'd give it up!" He turned to Dr. Von Durfull. "You positive they took it?" he said. "You scientists are a fuzzy-headed bunch, you know. First time I ever saw you, I said to myself, 'Now, there's a fella that's lost his buttons!' Maybe you just misplaced this one along with the others."

"Vatch out who you calling a button-loser!" Von Durfull replied sharply. "Anybody dot lets a live frog jump up his pants leg ain't got no right to call *anybody* a button-loser!"

"Then if they ain't got it they know where it is," the king said, indicating the Monkees. He motioned to the guards. "Take 'em to the torture chamber," he commanded. "I'll find that button or know the reason why!"

"We can stay right here and find out the reason why," Mike said. "One of those geese swallowed it."

The king looked at him reproachfully. "That's pret-ty low, fella," he said, "tryin' to blame a heinous crime like this on a poor little ol' goose. Ain't you got no shame?"

Mike began searching his pockets. "I had it

when I left the castle," he said. "Maybe I left it in the tower." He started toward the castle. "You-all wait here. I'll go look for it."

"Grab 'im!" the king shouted to the guards. The guards grabbed not only Mike but also Davy, Micky, and Peter. The whole group then set out for the torture chamber, which was next door to the dungeon.

As they passed the dungeon, the guard with the cavity spoke to the Monkees. "Gonna get tortured for somethin', eh?" he said. "I knew that long hair'd get you in trouble."

The torture chamber was a large room fitted out with every outmoded means of torture imaginable. There was a casket, so short that, once inside it, the prisoner was unable to stretch out. And a feather duster for tickling the bottoms of a prisoner's bare feet. And a Coke machine that took dimes but did not provide Cokes.

"That one," King Hiram said, indicating Davy. "Put 'im on the rack!"

The guards seized Davy and placed him, face up, on an apparatus that looked somewhat like a bed frame. His arms were stretched out over his head and secured. Then his legs were treated in a like manner.

74

"This isn't bad at all," Davy said. "Except that usually I sleep on my right side."

"You get one last chance, fella," King Hiram said. "Tell me what you done with that button."

Davy shook his head. "Not before I try out the rack first," he said. "I might like it."

"You know what that infernal machine does?" the king asked. "One end of it pulls on your arms and the other end of it pulls on your legs. And somethin's got to give. You can guess what happens."

"The machine comes apart?" Davy guessed.

"That's close—but not it," the king replied. He signaled to one of the guards. "Show him," he commanded.

The guard began turning a crank. Slowly, the head end of the rack started separating from the foot end. Davy, in the middle, was being stretched in both directions.

"Davy! Don't suffer!" Micky cried. "Confess!"

"Are you kidding?" Davy replied. "This is great! I've always wanted to be taller!"

"Hold it!" King Hiram shouted to the guard. "This ain't workin' out right. He ain't supposed to like it! Get that troublemaker off there!"

"Just a couple more turns," Davy pleaded as

the guard started to release him. "Please! I want to be taller than she is!"

"Take him off!" the king insisted. "I can't stand to hear a boy suffer like that." He turned to Smith. "How're we gonna get the truth out of these rascals?" he asked.

Smith grinned evilly. "Truth serum, perhaps, Your Highness."

"Why didn't I think of that?" the king asked.

"Probably because truth serum is too new-fangled and there isn't a drop of it in the whole kingdom," Smith replied.

"Well, I never thought we'd have any need for the truth," King Hiram said. "We've got along pretty good, so far, without it. Have you got any other ideas?"

"Fortunately, there's no need for that," Smith replied. He reached inside his cape and brought out a hypodermic needle. "I got some supplies from the drugstore before I left the U.S.," he explained. "Aspirin, cough syrup, and truth serum."

"I'll take one of the aspirin," King Hiram said, "and"—he pointed to Peter—"you can give him the truth serum."

"If it's all the same, I'd just as soon have the cough syrup," Peter said.

But, grinning evilly, Smith advanced on him with the needle.

"Hey! That looks sharp!" Peter protested, backing away.

Micky stepped forward. "I'll handle this," he said. "I didn't get those straight *A*'s in karate for nothing!"

"What did you get straight *A*'s for?" Mike asked.

"I was the teacher's pet," Micky replied. "He liked me because I didn't go around breaking boards like all the other students."

As Smith neared him, Micky delivered a karate chop to Smith's wrist. The needle dropped to the floor.

"Owwwwwww! That hurt!" Micky cried, holding his karate hand.

Peter quickly picked up the needle. *"Owwwww!"* he cried, holding his needle hand.

"But I'm the one who got hurt," Micky said accusingly.

"You're not the only one," Peter replied. "I jabbed myself with that needle."

"Now!" King Hiram shouted exultantly. "We'll get the truth!" He and Smith closed in on Peter. "Here's a sample question," the king said. "If

Peter Piper packed his purple pockets with pickled parsnips, how many sea shells did Sister Susie sink in the sand?"

"I cannot tell a lie," Peter replied. "I don't know."

"We're gettin' somewhere." King Hiram beamed. "That's the truth if I ever heard it. Now, here's the sixty-four-egg question," he said to Peter. "Where is The Button?"

"A goose swallowed it," Peter answered.

King Hiram shook a fist at the Monkees. "You lyin' no-goods!" he shouted angrily. "You were tellin' the truth all the time!" He signaled to the guards. "Lock 'em in their cell again," he ordered. Then he turned to Smith. "There's a traitor in our barnyard!" he said. "We'll string 'im up!"

"He's got the neck for it," Davy commented agreeably.

The king and Smith rushed off. The guards escorted the Monkees back to the dungeon.

Their jailer was not at all surprised to see them again.

"What're you in for this time?" he asked.

"As I understand it, for telling the truth," Micky replied.

The guard shook his head in disgust. "You guys

79

with long hair won't stop at nothin'," he said. He opened the cell door. "Inside!"

The Monkees settled gloomily on the cot in the cell and watched silently as the guard began patrolling back and forth in front of the cells.

"What're we going to do now?" Mike asked.

"Make another mistake," Peter replied.

The others looked at him.

"I'm still under the influence of the truth serum," he explained. "Anybody want to know who cut down the cherry tree? I cannot tell a lie—George Washington did it. But, of course, that was a long time ago. He was only a little kid. I think it's unfair to keep bringing it up again and again and again, every time he has a birthday. How would you like it if, every time you had a birthday, everybody kept reminding you about some kid trick you pulled? You'd get a complex, that's what. You'd drop out of school and turn to vandalism. One thing for sure, you'd never grow up to be President. You'd end up peddling secondhand comic books from door to door, just like George Washington did."

"George Washington did become President," Micky pointed out.

Peter frowned. "I thought that was Abe Lincoln." He shrugged. "I never could keep them straight."

"We sure could use another cake to bribe that guard," Mike said.

"Let's call room service and see if we can get one sent down," Davy suggested.

Mike considered for a moment. "It's worth a try," he decided. He got up and went to the bars and motioned to the guard. "Can I use your phone?" he asked.

The guard looked around, frightened. *"Shhhh!* Nobody knows about that," he said. "How'd you find out about it?"

"About what?" Mike asked blankly.

"About my phone. Phones aren't allowed in Bellevue. If the king knew I had one, he'd put me on the rack!"

"I'll take your place," Davy volunteered.

"If you have the only phone in the country, what good is it?" Mike asked.

"Just my way of relaxin'," the guard replied. "On Sunday, instead of going to the band concert, I stay home and make calls. I call Alleppey, India; and Banja Luka, Yugoslavia; and Chengting, China; and Dungarvin, Ireland; and Embabaan, Switzerland; and all kinds of places."

"You sure must have quite a phone bill," Mike said.

"No bill. The phone ain't hooked up."

"In that case, I withdraw my request," Mike said, returning to the cot.

"We'll just have to wait for Princess Ellie Jo to bring us more eggs," Peter said.

"She won't show," Davy said. "We're losers again."

"She'll be here in about three seconds," Peter insisted.

"How can you be so sure?" Micky asked.

"Beats me," Peter replied. "That was the truth serum talking."

Exactly three seconds later, Princess Ellie Jo appeared again at the cell door. She was carrying a large handbag.

"Land o' goshen! Fancy meetin' you here!" she said to the Monkees, blushing. "I was just passin' this way. I sure enough never expected to find you four handsome troubadours behind bars again. You been cuttin' fancy capers again, you naughties?"

"Will you just hand over the cake?" Mike replied.

The princess lowered her voice. "They're all

out of twenty-four eggers at the bakery," she answered. "I had to bring cash this time." She opened the handbag and brought out an egg carton. "It's in this wallet," she said, passing the carton through the bars. "Hide it somewheres."

Micky took the carton from her hand. "Wallet?" he said, perplexed. He stuffed it into his rear pocket. "What happened to the guard?" he asked her.

"He's outside holdin' my horse," Princess Ellie Jo explained. "I didn't want him to overhear what I got to tell you. There's still a chance for you boys to latch onto that button."

"You mean your father hasn't found the goose yet?" Mike asked.

"He ain't found no goose a-tall," the princess replied. "He wasted so much time torturin' you boys, when he got up to the barnyard all the geese were gone. They'd been sent off to market."

"What's he doing now?" Micky asked.

"Sittin'. He figured out a way to get them geese back. He put out a royal decree sayin' that henceforth all the geese in the country are royal geese and royal geese can't be butchered."

"I don't see how that will solve the problem," Mike said.

"Bein' royal geese, all the geese in the country are bein' brought to the castle," the princess replied. "When they all get here, Paw's gonna butcher 'em."

"And find The Button." Mike nodded.

"Won't that be against the law?" Peter asked judicially.

"That's the thing about law in Bellevue," the princess replied. "Paw can make it, and he can break it. When it suits him, I reckon he'll find a way to break it, all right."

"We've got to get out of here!" Mike said.

"Why?" Davy asked. "If King Hiram has all the geese, what can we do?"

"I don't know," Mike replied. "I just thought it was the right thing to say at the time."

"It was right, sugar," Princess Ellie Jo said. "Paw don't have all them geese yet. A lot of 'em ain't been brought in yet. In fact, only one or two. Folks are butcherin' geese right and left and sayin' they done it six months ago 'fore they heard about any law. So that goose that's got The Button is probably still out there somewheres."

"We've got to get out of here!" Mike said again. He turned to Davy. "How was that? Better for timing?"

84

"Perfect."

"I'm leavin' now," Princess Ellie Jo said. "I don't like to be seen too long in the company of losers. You sure you know what to do?"

"We bribe the guard, escape, then rush to the marketplace and find the goose that swallowed The Button. Right?" Mike said.

The princess frowned. "That worries me—you got it right the first time," she said. "The mistake, I'm feared, is yet to come." She moved on. "Well, when you get mixed up with losers. . . ." She sighed.

When she was gone, the Monkees returned to the cot and waited for the guard to come back. He reappeared a few minutes later.

"I was out holdin' the princess's horse," he said proudly to the Monkees. "That's quite an honor, holdin' the princess's horse. I sure will have somethin' to tell the folks in Alleppey, India, this Sunday."

Mike got up and walked to the bars. "How would you like to visit those good friends of yours in Alleppey, India, that you never get to talk to on the phone?" he asked. "A thing like that could be arranged if you just had enough eggs, couldn't it?"

The guard looked at him suspiciously. "Are you offerin' me a bribe?" he asked.

"Look at this long hair—what else would I be doing?" Mike replied.

"Don't you know that bribin' a royal guard is a naughty, naughty, *naughty* thing to do?" the guard said. "If it wasn't for all my good friends in Alleppey, India, dyin' to meet me, I just might report you to the king. How much're you offerin'?"

Mike faced back to the others. "Count the eggs," he said to Micky.

"I don't think I can do that," Micky replied. "But, one thing, I'm sure there're more of them now than when we got them."

"Why can't you count them?" Mike asked.

"Remember where I put the wallet?" Mike replied.

"In your hip pocket."

"And remember what I did then?"

"You went back to the cot and sat—" Mike turned back to the guard. "How far can you go on scrambled eggs in this country?" he asked brokenly.

"About as far as from where you're standin' to where you're standin'," the guard answered.

"I was afraid of that. Look, can you come back

a little later for that bribe? Right now, we're broke."

"I can wait," the guard said. "It's them good folks in Alleppey, India, that it's gonna be tough on."

Mike returned to the cot. Micky got the wallet from his back pocket and opened it, and all of the Monkees huddled around to see exactly how much damage had been done to the eggs.

"Ugh!" Davy said, summing up the opinion of the group.

"It couldn't be as bad as it looks," Mike said. "Maybe we can piece some of them together."

"There aren't enough good eggs here to pay that guard's phone bill," Micky said.

"We can try, can't we?" Mike argued. He picked up a half-shell. "Where does this fit?"

The guard called in to them from the corridor. "You'll never get anywhere that way," he advised. "You got to have a system." He opened the door and entered the cell. "Let me show you."

"You mean this has happened to you?" Davy said.

"Sure. I sit down on my wallet all the time. Most when I'm usin' the phone. I get a cramp in my left leg when I stand too long." He handed his gun to Peter. "Hold this," he said. "I got to have both hands free."

Peter passed the gun to Mike. "You hold it; I want to watch," he said.

Mike, in turn, handed the weapon to Micky.

"I don't want it," Micky complained.

"Oh, all right, give it back!" the guard said irritably. "I don't even know why I'm tryin' to help you; you won't even hold my gun for me." He took the gun from Micky and leaned it against the cell wall. "Now, let's see . . ." he said, studying the mess in the wallet. "First, we got to separate all the big pieces from the itsy-bitsy pieces. Just stand back. Give me room to operate. . . ."

The Monkees moved away, giving the guard more room.

" 'Course, you understand, I could do a better job of it if I had me one of them X rays the king won't allow in the country," the guard said. "I could sort of see how the grain goes. Then I could fit the rough edges. . . . Well, no sense wishin' for what ain't. Now, if one of you boys'll just hold onto this big hunk right here for a minute. . . ." He handed a large piece of shell back toward the Monkees.

But no one took it from him.

WHO'S GOT THE BUTTON?

The guard turned and looked behind him. The Monkees were gone.

"Dagnabit!" he grumbled. "When I said 'stand back,' I didn't nohow mean *that* far back!"

5

Black Market Bargains

THE MONKEES SAUNTERED nonchalantly from the dungeon. Reaching the main floor of the castle, they spotted a guard patrolling the corridor.

"How will we get past him?" Mike whispered.

Micky got out his tour guide cap, put it on, and motioned for the others to follow.

"And on our left, folks, we have the Great Wall of China. Notice, in particular, the cups and saucers," Micky chanted, leading the tour along the corridor.

The guard, sighting them, eyed the group speculatively.

90

"And here," Micky said as they reached the guard, "we have probably the most interesting sight on the whole tour. Pay special attention to this guard's disposition. See how amiable he appears to be."

"What's goin' on here?" the guard roared.

"See that!" Micky said. "First he was amiable; now he's angry. That's what we call 'The Changing of the Guard!' "

"No tours allowed!" the guard shouted.

"Fascinating! He speaks in sign language," Mike said.

"Out!" the guard raged.

"Right this way, folks," Micky continued, leading the way toward the exit. "Up ahead, we have the Great Outdoors. You've read about it in books, and now you'll see it in person. As you step out the door, sniff the fresh air. Not canned, not frozen—but fresh! Guaranteed to take the fall out of your arches, put spring in your step, and keep your winter green!"

"Is every day's air like that in Bellevue?" Davy asked.

Micky shook his head. "Summer and summer not."

The moment they were outside the castle, Micky

took off his tour guide cap. "Which way to the marketplace?" he asked. "I can't find my way around a corner when I'm out of uniform."

"We'd better ask directions," Davy said.

"There he is over there," Peter said, pointing to a man who was leaning against a hitching post.

The Monkees approached the man. "Mr. Directions?" Mike asked, extending a hand.

"That's right—Sam Directions, at your service," the man replied, shaking Mike's hand. "Always nice to meet somebody who's lost. How would you like to get to Battery Park from the Bronx by way of Tenafly, New Jersey? That's my special for today."

"No, thanks," Mike replied. "All we'd—"

"Malibu Beach by way of the San Francisco Bay Bridge?" Directions broke in. "That one's left over from the Republican Convention of '64. You can have it cheap."

"We just want to get to the marketplace," Mike answered.

"Well, you take a hansom cab to the border, cross over into the next country, hitch a ride to the airport, fly to Alleppey, India—"

"Never mind," Mike interrupted. "We'll find it ourselves."

The Monkees moved on to the curb and began looking for a hansom cab.

"There's one!" Peter said.

Micky shook his head. "Comely—but not hansom," he said. "We'd better wait."

An ugly cab passed. Then a spruce cab. Then a charming cab. Finally, a hansom cab appeared, and the Monkees halted it and clambered aboard.

"To the marketplace!" Mike said to the driver.

The driver cracked his whip and the horse broke into a gallop. Several blocks later they reached a crowded area of shops. The sidewalks were thronged with shoppers, all carrying large baskets of eggs. The driver pulled the horse to a stop and the Monkees jumped out.

"That'll be one egg," the driver said.

"Ah . . . we seem to be a little short," Mike replied.

"I can believe that about him," the driver said, pointing to Davy. "But what about the rest of you?"

"Would you take me instead?" Micky asked. "I've always been known as a pretty good egg."

The driver studied him a moment and then replied, "Let's call it even. With you up here in the seat with me, I wouldn't have a hansom cab anymore. Try me again, though, if you ever get your hair cut."

The driver snapped his whip again, and once more the horse galloped off.

The Monkees began going from shop to shop trying to find geese, so that by the process of elimination they would find the goose that had swallowed The Button. But it appeared that they were too late. In every shop they were told that the geese had been taken to the castle.

Finally, however, one friendly shopkeeper drew them aside and whispered, "There's only one place in the whole country—besides the castle—that might still have a goose. Try the Black Market!"

"Where is it?" Mike whispered back.

"Around in the alley," the shopkeeper replied. "You can't miss it. There's a big sign over the door, saying BLACK MARKET."

The Monkees thanked the shopkeeper. They rushed from the shop and ran to the alley behind the buildings. As soon as they entered the alley they saw the sign. It said:

BLACK MARKET
Fred Black, Prop.

The Monkees dashed inside, and were met by

a large, roly-poly, smiling man who was wearing a straw hat and a butcher's apron.

"We were told we might find some geese here," Mike said hopefully.

Fred Black looked them over. "Plainclothes cops, eh?" he replied. "You won't find any geese here, boys. I know the law—all the geese go to the castle. Do I look like a man that'd break the law?" He lowered his voice. "Who snitched on me?" he asked. "Somebody that bought a goose from me and found a horn in its craw, I'll bet!"

"We're not police, we're customers," Mike replied. "And what do you mean, a horn in its craw?"

"Where do you think those honks come from?" Black asked. "You think every time a goose makes a noise it's just coincidence that a car's passing by? Well, you're right. That's what the noise is in other countries. But here in Bellevue we don't have any cars. So we have to fit out our geese with horns of their own. Customers, eh?" He beamed. "What can I sell you that is against the law to sell you? How about a brand-new telephone? Never been used. Imported from Alleppey, India."

"We're looking for geese," Micky said.

"Funny thing you should mention geese," Black

replied. "I just got in a big shipment of geese. The minute I heard there was a law against it, I stocked up."

"If all the geese are going to the castle, where do you get your geese?" Davy asked.

"Where else? From the castle," Black replied. "The people take their geese to the front door, and I get them from the Royal Geese Receiver at the back door. Business is a two-way street, you know. The people take their geese up First Avenue, and I bring them back along Second Avenue. And everybody wins. The people obey the law by turning in their geese. Then they come here and buy them back. That way, they can have their cake and eat it, too."

"Where does the cake come in?" Peter asked, interested.

"I make them buy a cake when they get their geese," Black explained. "That's where the profit is. Oh, this goose business is fascinating, all right. The stories I could tell! You wouldn't believe them. But, I'll give you a chance, anyway. I've got thirty-two dozen geese in the back room, all butchered and ready for the oven. Now, that's pretty unbelievable in itself. But—would you believe it?—that's not the fascinating part. What's really interesting is the things I found in those geese when I butchered them. They talk about goats eating strange and uncommon objects. But a goose! Wow! Guess what I found in the first goose I opened up."

"A goat?" Peter guessed.

Black frowned. "Have you heard this story before?"

"Never," Peter replied. "That was just a wild goose."

"Well, to make a short story shorter," Black went on, "some of the things I've found in geese, in the order of their appearance, are a left-handed crank for a right-handed ice cream freezer, a giant tiddlywink, ticket stubs to the opening performance of *Abie's Irish Rose,* a button, four—"

"A button!" the Monkees cried in unison.

Black looked at them warily. "You think a button is stranger than a left-handed crank?" he said. "You sure you're not plainclothes cops?"

"What did this button look like?" Mike asked.

"Like it was sewed to a hip pocket," Black replied. "I was going to mention the hip pocket later."

"Just to be sure. . . . Was this button red?" Mike asked. "Pink? Blue?"

"You're close," Mike said. "But not close enough."

"Was it black?"

Black shook his head. "Gray with two holes in the middle," he replied. "It's the giant tiddlywink that's black." He opened a drawer and got out a round, black object and placed it on the counter. "Ever see a giant tiddlywink as big as that before?" he asked proudly. "I'll get a basket of eggs for it from some giant tiddlywink collector."

"The Button!" the Monkees cried in unison.

Black looked at The Button closely. "What kind of a button is that? No holes." He picked it up and dropped it back into the drawer. "But, no matter. As they say: One man's tiddlywink is another man's button. Now then, about what size goose were you looking for?"

"Actually, we're more interested in The Button," Mike said. "Is it for sale?"

"Maybe," Black replied cagily. "Will you take the hip pocket with it?"

"No, not that button," Mike replied. "The button you call a giant tiddlywink."

"Oh, you mean that giant tiddlywink that you boys call a button." He shook his head. "I couldn't sell that," he replied. "It's been in the family for hours. I wouldn't feel right about taking eggs for it. I'll give it to you, though, for free."

"Amazing!" Micky said. "That's exactly what we can afford!"

Mike put out a hand. "Handle it gently, please, and put it right there," he said.

"In a minute," Black replied. "First, I'll get your cake for you. What good would a button be without a cake to go with it?"

"Am I right in assuming that the cake is the catch?" Mike asked.

Black scowled. "You'll have to be a little more specific," he replied.

"In other words," Mike said, "am I right in assuming that you won't give us The Button unless we buy the cake?"

"You were right the first time. The cake is the catch," Black replied. "Angel food or devil's food?"

"How much?" Micky asked.

"I like you—only four dozen eggs," Black answered.

"If we stuck around awhile, do you think you could grow to hate us a little?" Micky asked.

"How could I do a thing like that to somebody I like?" Black replied.

Mike motioned the others into a huddle and they conferred. "Where're we going to get four dozen eggs on short notice?" he asked.

"Let's try the bank," Peter said. "If we tell them we can get a giant tiddlywink for it, they'll be glad to give us a loan. A collector will pay a basket of eggs for a giant tiddlywink."

"We'll try it," Mike decided. "We couldn't be any worse off after being kicked out of a bank than we are now." Breaking from the huddle, he returned to where Black was waiting. "Hold onto that tiddlywink," he said. "We'll be back in a flash with the cash."

"Don't be too long," Black warned. "There's a big market for tiddlywinks or buttons or whatever that thing is these days."

The Monkees left the Black Market, emerged from the alley, then entered the nearest bank. The guard at the door directed them to the officer in charge of loans, who was seated at a desk at the rear of the bank.

"We want to talk to you about a loan," Mike said when they reached the man.

"Wonderful!" the man replied, obviously relieved. "On my salary, I can hardly make ends meet. How much can you give me?"

"I think you've got it a little turned around," Mike replied. "We want to borrow from you."

"Oh . . . that again," the man said dismally. He sighed. "All right. But I'll have to get some information from you." He got a form from a drawer of the desk. "How much do you want to borrow?" he asked.

"Four dozen eggs," Mike answered.

"Ummmm . . . got your eye on a giant tiddlywink, eh?" the man said knowingly. "Okay. Now, what have you got for collateral?"

"What does *he* want?" Davy asked.

"Collateral isn't a he, it's an it," the man replied. "It's what you have that's worth more than four dozen eggs that we can take away from you if you fail to repay the four dozen eggs."

"How about the giant tiddlywink?" suggested Peter.

The loan officer shook his head. "That's worth four dozen eggs exactly," he said. "The collateral will have to be worth more."

"Then how about a button that will give us absolute and total control over the whole world?" Micky asked.

The loan officer thought a moment and then nodded. "That ought to be worth five dozen eggs, at least," he said. "Now, then, can you describe this button? New or used?"

"New," Mike answered. "If it were used there wouldn't be any world left to control."

"Very good," the man said. He turned the form toward Mike. "Sign on the dotted line," he said.

"Whose name?" Mike asked.

"Somebody rich," the loan officer replied. "It looks better to the brass that way."

"I'll just sign the bank's name," Mike said. "I'll bet it's loaded."

"Good," the loan officer agreed. "That'll make a big impression in the head office." He opened another desk drawer and got out four one-dozen cartons of eggs and handed them to Micky. "Just don't eat any of them," he warned. "I've had them in that drawer for six months."

With Micky carrying the cartons, the Monkees headed toward the exit. But just as they reached the door, the guard called out to them.

"Halt!" he said. "What've you got in them cartons?"

"Eggs," Micky replied innocently.

"I'll just take a look at that," the guard said suspiciously. He opened one of the cartons and peeked in. "Eggs!" he said, surprised. "Sorry, boys. But I've got to keep a sharp eye out. A lot of nice folks like you come in here and steal our pens and try to smuggle 'em out in egg cartons."

"We borrowed these eggs, all upright and above-board," Mike said. "We put up a button as the collateral."

"Hey! Pretty good deal!" the guard said, impressed.

"Yeah, it was a steal," Micky replied.

The Monkees moved on.

"A steal!" the guard shouted suddenly. "Stop! Thieves! Bank robbery!"

A whistle blew! A gun fired!

"Do you think we ought to go back and explain?" Davy asked.

"Sure, we can show him how we got the eggs by signing the bank's name to the loan," Peter said.

"Let's run first and explain later," Mike decided.

The Monkees dashed from the bank—and right into the arms of a dozen policemen.

"Where's the bank robbery?" one of the policeman asked.

Davy pointed back into the bank. "We were in there when we heard about it," he answered.

The policemen rushed on into the bank.

The Monkees started up the street, taking their time, not wanting to draw attention. But a moment later the policemen came running back out of the bank. They were accompanied by the guard.

"That's them! I got their confession!" the guard shouted, pointing out the Monkees.

The Monkees began taking their time at a much faster pace.

"Why are we running?" Micky asked, clinging to the cartons of eggs. "We didn't do anything illegal."

A shot was fired! A bullet zinged past them!

"That explains it," Micky said.

The Monkees raced from the marketplace, then up a narrow street, down a wide avenue, up a narrow alley, and down a wide boulevard. The guard and the police, meanwhile, still firing, raced from the marketplace, then up a wide boulevard, down a narrow alley, up a wide avenue, and down a narrow street. At that point, the Monkees and the guard and the policemen all met.

"How's about across a bridge this time?" Davy suggested.

"Fine by me," the guard replied. "How's about it by you boys?" he asked the policemen.

"This is your chase," the head policeman said

105

to the guard and the Monkees. "Anything you decide is okay by us."

"Over the bridge and through the woods it is, then," Davy said. "And we'll all meet at Grandmother's house. Okay?"

Without waiting for a reply, the Monkees took off again. And the guard and the policeman set out once more to catch them, firing their guns and shouting, "Stop, thieves! Stop, thieves!" all the while.

Reaching the bridge, the Monkees started across. Unfortunately, it was a drawbridge, and, just as they set foot on it, it began rising up in the middle to allow a boat to pass underneath.

"We probably should go back," Mike said.

"And be late getting to Grandmother's house?" Peter said. "The guard and those policemen would never forgive us."

"Onward!" Mike pointed.

The Monkees charged up the bridge, reached the center, and plunged downward over the edge.

Looking down and seeing a barge, Davy said, "I think we're going to be late getting to Grandmother's house anyway. That boat is going in the opposite direction."

"You know something worse?" Micky said.

Mike nodded. "We're going to be killed," he said.

"Even worse than that," Micky said. "We're going to lose our entire fortune. Did you ever hear of an egg falling off the end of a bridge and landing on a barge and surviving?"

"Let me think." Mike frowned. "I may have and I may not have. If you'll just give me a min—"

His thoughts were interrupted. At that instant the Monkees and the cartons of eggs hit the barge. Luckily, however, it was not an ordinary barge. It was owned and operated by a group of Bellevuian college students who, as a prank, had kidnapped all the royal chickens, intending to hold them prisoner over the weekend. Being boys, though, the college students had soon become extremely hungry. And, wild from starvation, they had set upon the royal chickens. Consequently, what the Monkees and the cartons of eggs landed on was the remains: a soft bed of thousands and thousands of chicken feathers.

"Saved by the machinations of a group of well-meaning but misguided college students!" the Monkees cried joyfully in unison as they landed in a cloud of feathers.

"I think we cried joyfully in unison too soon,"

Mike said, pointing. "Look! The guard and the police have commandeered a rowboat. They're coming after us!"

"But can they catch us?" Davy postulated.

"They're a cinch," Mike replied. "They can row faster than we can barge."

"Then let's commandeer a lifeboat and row back to shore," Davy said. "They can't row faster than we can row, because there are four of us and there are only seven of them."

"That doesn't make sense," Mike pointed out.

"Certainly it does. With so many of them in that little rowboat some of them are bound to get in the way and slow the others up."

"That does make sense," Mike said, surprised.

Quickly, the Monkees jumped into a lifeboat, lowered it to the water, and then rowed toward shore. The guard and the policemen immediately changed course to follow them.

The Monkees' boat reached land first, however. And while the guard and the policemen were still yards from shore, the Monkees jumped from their boat and rushed toward the marketplace.

Mike was the first to reach Black's market. He dashed in and, panting, said to the proprietor, "The eggs are coming!"

NO WADING
—
SWIMMING
O.K.

"Good, good," Black replied, rubbing his hands together greedily.

Peter was next to arrive. "The eggs are coming, all four dozen of them!" he announced, panting.

At that same moment, Davy burst through the doorway. "The eggs—" he began.

"I know, I know," Black broke in. "Let's have less talk and more do."

Then Micky appeared, carrying the four cartons of eggs in his arms. "Here are—" he said. Then he interrupted himself long enough to trip over the sill of the door and fall flat on top of the cartons. There were four dozen cracking sounds.

From his position atop the cartons, Micky looked up hopefully at Black. "It won't bother you, will it, if it's in small change?" he asked.

"The deal is off," Black replied. "I'd sound like a weirdo walking around with four dozen eggs in change jangling in my pocket."

At that instant, a small, yellow, fuzzy head poked out from beneath Micky. It looked remarkably like the head of a baby chick. Then the chick spoke, removing all doubt.

"Peep!" it said.

Micky jumped up. "I'm a mother!" he cried, panic-stricken.

Where Micky had been, forty-seven additional baby chicks now appeared.

"Congratulations, little mother," Mike said to Micky. "Besides eggs, you've broken every record in the books. You've had quintuplets nine and three-fifths times in one day."

"The deal is on again!" Black cried excitedly. He ran to the counter, yanked open the drawer, got The Button, and ran back to Mike, slapping it into the palm of his hand and closing his fingers around it. "A deal is a deal!" he insisted. "You get this valuable giant tiddlywink and I get those four dozen worthless chickens!"

"I don't think I quite understand this," Mike said.

"You're too sharp for me; you outwitted me," Black replied.

"We accept the deal—on one condition," Mike said. "Tell us the truth. Why are you willing to accept four dozen broken eggs?"

"Those four dozen broken eggs are going to grow up to be four dozen egg-laying chickens," Black explained. "Another few months and I'll have the only black market mint on the block. I'll be—"

There was a sudden loud pounding at the door.

"The guard and the police!" Davy said. "They caught up with us!"

"Quick!" Black said. "Out the front door!"

"You mean the back door, don't you?" Micky asked.

"My shop is in the alley," Black replied. "So that makes my back door my front door, and my front door my back door. That pounding is at my front door, which is my back door, so you want out my back door, which is my front door."

"Is there a side door?" Mike asked. "That would be a little less confusing."

"No good," Black replied. "It leads to the basement." He rushed to the door at the rear of the market. "This way," he urged, opening it wide.

The Monkees raced past him and out into the street—and straight into the clutches of a squad of the king's soldiers. Behind them, the door of the market slammed shut.

6

Scrambled Justice

Boy, THAT WAS close!" Davy said. "Another minute and we'd have been arrested for bank robbing." He looked up at the king's soldier who was holding him. "What are you arresting us for?" he asked.

It was the leader of the soldiers who replied. "We're taking you in for jail breaking," he answered.

"You've got the wrong guys," Mike said. "You want somebody with a sledgehammer. We're just not equipped for breaking a jail."

"You're the ones we want, all right," the leader said. "I recognize the hair."

At that instant, the door of the market flew open again. The bank guard and the policemen came charging out. And, spotting the Monkees, they quickly seized them.

"Gotcha!" the bank guard announced victoriously. "You're under arrest for bank robbing!"

"Hold on, there!" the leader of the soldiers objected. "I arrested them first. They're coming with me!"

"Who says?" the bank guard replied belligerently. "I arrested them about an hour ago. Maybe I only caught up with them just now, but that don't change the fact that I was the first to arrest them. They're coming with me!"

"Oh, yeah!" the leader of the soldiers said. "Well, let me tell you—"

"Now, just a minute," Mike said soothingly. "I'm sure this can be settled without resorting to angry words." He addressed the bank guard. "What's the penalty for bank robbing?" he asked.

"Thirty years."

"And for jail breaking?" Mike asked the leader of the soldiers.

"Life—if you live that long," the soldier replied.

"Then doesn't that make it obvious?" Mike said. "The bank guard arrested us first. In fact, I have witnesses." He turned to the other Monkees. "Who arrested us first—thirty years or life?"

"Their word's no good!" the leader of the soldiers broke in before the other Monkees could reply. "It's common knowledge that a criminal will lie to save himself from going to jail for life. That's what makes a criminal different from honest folks."

"I'd take the word of a criminal 'fore I'd take the word of a soldier!" the bank guard shouted.

The leader of the soldiers pulled back a fist. "No four-egg-a-week bank guard is going to talk to me like that!" he said. "I'll knock you right out from under your three o'clock closing time!"

"Yah! Yah! Soldiers wear army boots!" the guard sneered.

Again, Mike intervened. "We're wasting a lot of time while we could be in jail for one reason or another," he protested. "Can't we take this problem to some higher authority and get it settled without a fight?"

"Good idea," the bank guard said. "We'll go ask my mother who's right." Then he changed his mind. "No," he decided, "she'd side with him. Mom's a pushover for an army uniform." Then he brightened. "We'll go over Mom's head—straight to the Supreme Court!"

"I accept that," the leader of the soldiers said. "I'm not worried about the verdict. Right is on my side. And, if I don't win that way, I can always overthrow the country and kick out the Court. Maybe soldiering don't pay much, but having the guns makes it worth it." He raised an arm. "On to the Court!"

The Monkees, the bank guard, the policemen, and the soldiers entered the Supreme Court building, proceeded to the courtroom, and then approached the bench.

The judge, who looked remarkably like King Hiram, eyed them irritably. "What're all you dingdong boys doin' here?" he asked crankily. "The bank guard's mother's supposed to hear the cases 'fore I get 'em."

"There's no time for that, Your Honor," the bank guard replied. "These criminals are in a hurry to get to jail."

"Pushy, eh?" the judge said to the Monkees. "You must be foreigners. That's two strikes against you right there. Sure you want to go through with the rest of the trial?"

"Your Honor, we are not on trial," Micky replied.

"I'll decide that!" the judge roared. He addressed the bank guard and the leader of the soldiers. "What's the question before the court?" he asked. "And make it short—these criminals are in a hurry to get to jail."

"The question is," the bank guard replied, "who arrested the criminals first, me or the soldiers? Now, I don't want to influence the court in any way, but I would like to point out that I have considerable influence at the bank—in case the judge would care to borrow a large sum of eggs and forget to pay it back."

"I object!" the leader of the soldiers shouted.

"To that attempt to bribe me?" the judge asked.

"No, to the way he put the question," the leader of the soldiers replied. "Actually, the question is, why did he claim to be the first to arrest the criminals when he knew all along that, in fact, I was the first?"

"I object to that objection!" the bank guard objected.

The judge banged his gavel. "Order in the court!" he roared. "Since we can't agree on the question, we'll just skip it and proceed with the proceedin's." Again he banged the gavel. "I'm ready to announce the verdict," he said. "I find the defendants guilty as charged. Now, let's get on with the trial. Bank guard, call your last witness!"

"Just a minute," Davy interrupted. "If you've already reached a verdict, Your Honor, why go on with the trial?"

"To find out *how* I reached it," the judge replied. "We need all that in-between stuff for the records."

"As my last witness, I call this one," the bank guard said, indicating Micky. "Take the stand, young man."

"That's stealing," Micky said. "I'm in enough trouble as it is, robbing a bank and breaking jail."

"See how honest and upright he is, Judge?" The bank guard smiled. "That's proof positive that you can trust his testimony."

"Not likely," the judge grumbled. "He can tell the truth all he wants to, but I'll know he's lyin'. I can see that long hair!"

The bank guard whispered to Micky. "Shorten your hair," he said. "It'll make a good impression on the judge."

"I can't," Micky whispered back. "It just grows this way."

"Get it to squat down a little."

"Stop coachin' the witness!" the judge shouted, banging his gavel again. "Proceed with the questionin' at once!"

"Be seated, witness," the bank guard said.

Micky settled in the witness chair.

"All right, ask me anything," the bank guard said. "Anything at all. My whole life is an open book."

Micky leaned forward. His eyes narrowed. "Now, think before you answer this," he said. "I'm warning you, it's a trick question. Ready?"

"Shoot!"

"Here's the question," Micky said. "Who's your little whozit? Who's the one you love? Who's your little whozit? Who's your turtledove?"

"Shucks, that's easy," the bank guard replied. "It's Mom."

"Stop!" the leader of the soldiers suddenly shouted in anguish. "I can't stand it!" he sobbed. "You're destroying a fine human being with your savage interrogation! I confess! I did it!"

"That was a trickier question than I thought," Micky said, surprised. "I expected the judge to confess."

The judge banged his gavel once more. "Now

we're gettin' somewhere," he said. "We know who did it. Let's find out what it was he did. Anybody got any ideas?"

"Let's ask him," Mike suggested, pointing to the leader of the guards. "He's the one who confessed."

"I object!" the bank guard said. "You know the old saying: Ask a tricky question and get a tricky answer. If he's allowed to answer, I'll lose the case."

"I demand the right to have my confession heard!" the leader of the soldiers said.

"All right, we'll hear it. But it'll be off-the-record," the judge said. "If we don't like it, we'll just pretend you didn't say it. What do you confess to?"

The leader of the soldiers smiled triumphantly. "I confess that I was the one who arrested the criminals first," he replied.

"The court didn't hear that," the judge ruled. "Proceed with the trial."

"I wish to call a character witness, Your Honor," the bank guard said. He pointed to Peter. "That one."

"That's a character, all right," the judge replied. "Request granted."

Micky stepped down and Peter took the stand.

"Bring that back here!" the judge raged.

Looking sheepish, Peter returned the stand. Then he sat down in the witness chair.

"How long have you known the defendants, young man?" the bank guard asked.

Peter spread his hands. "About that long," he answered.

"Long enough," the bank guard continued, "to know that, in spite of anything to the contrary that might be revealed in this courtroom, they are a bunch of no-good, low-down, good-for-nothin' bad guys?"

"Clear the court!" the judge shouted, banging his gavel angrily. "I won't have criminals like that in my courtroom! Get those no-goods out of here!"

"Heard enough evidence, eh, Judge?" The bank guard beamed.

"No, that has nothin' to do with it," the judge replied. "It's time for lunch. Let's see now," he said. "We've had the verdict, and we've had the trial. . . . How do we wind this thing up?"

"You read the charges against the defendants, Judge," the leader of the soldiers answered.

"That sounds familiar." The judge nodded. He

addressed the Monkees. "You are charged with gettin' yourselves arrested by both a bank guard and the police and the king's soldiers, thereby startin' an argument and creatin' a public disturbance." He rapped his gavel. "Case closed," he announced.

"We object!" the Monkees shouted in unison.

"What's your objection?" the judge asked sharply. "And make it snappy—you're on my lunch hour."

"We thought the guard and the police and the soldiers were on trial," Davy explained.

"Ignorance is no excuse," the judge ruled, pounding his gavel again. "Everybody out!"

The Monkees, the bank guard, the policemen, and the soldiers departed. They collected in a circle outside the Supreme Court building.

"How did it come out?" the bank guard asked the leader of the soldiers. "Who gets custody of the criminals?"

"All I know is, I was listening for the part where I won, and I didn't hear it," the leader of the soldiers replied.

"That's what I was listening for, too, and I didn't hear it, either." The bank guard sighed. "What do we do now?"

"Let's call it a draw and release the prisoners into their own custody," Davy suggested.

"That's not fair," the bank guard complained. "I ought to get them. I arrested them first."

"Says who!" the leader of the soldiers snapped. "I arrested them first."

The bank guard pulled back a fist. "How'd you like to get called a nasty name?" he demanded belligerently.

The leader of the soldiers pulled back a fist, too. "Oh, yeah! How'd you like to get kicked in the shins with an army boot?"

"I'll take this to the Supreme Court!" the bank guard threatened.

"Oh, no—not that again!" Mike protested. "There must be an easier and faster way. Let's flip a coin."

The bank guard and the leader of the soldiers peered at him, puzzled.

"A what?" they asked in unison.

"An egg," Mike replied.

"Good idea," the bank guard said. He got an egg from his pocket. "Big end or little end?" he asked the leader of the soldiers.

"Not so fast," the leader of the soldiers replied. "Let me see that egg."

The bank guard handed it over.

"Okay," the leader of the soldiers said, after inspecting it closely. "I just wanted to be sure it wasn't one of those trick eggs with two little ends and no big end. I've been caught on that one before." He pondered a moment, then said, "I'll take the big end."

"First, let's make sure there's no disagreement about the rules," Micky said. "Will the first toss decide it, or will it be two out of three?"

"When you toss an egg, there's no second chance," the leader of the soldiers replied.

"Here she goes!" the bank guard said.

He tossed the egg high into the air. Everybody stepped back. A moment later the egg hit the sidewalk and splattered. There was more of the big end left, however, than there was of the little end.

"Well, that's the way the egg splatters." The bank guard shrugged. "They're your prisoners," he said to the leader of the soldiers.

"Tell you what," the leader of the soldiers said. "As soon as they finish serving that life sentence for me, you can have them for the next thirty years."

"Well, thanks, anyway," the bank guard replied.

"But, by then, I'll probably be too old to enjoy it." He saluted smartly—a gesture signifying acceptance of defeat—and then he and the police departed.

There was obvious respect in the eyes of the leader of the soldiers as he watched the bank guard go. "It's an honor to win over a man like that," he said. "Or over anybody, for that matter," he added. He turned to the Monkees. "March!" he ordered. "Back to the cell with the lot of you!"

With soldiers in front of them and soldiers in back of them, the Monkees began the long trek back to the castle.

"You know—" Mike began.

"Are you going to be an alarmist again?" Peter asked.

"That's not my intention," Mike replied. "But still, I think we ought to recognize the fact that if we're going to jail for life, we're not going to get The Button back to Washington as soon as we had expected to."

"Is that all?" Davy said. "I was afraid you were going to point out that as soon as we get back to the castle the king will probably have us frisked and will find The Button."

"Yi!" Micky cried. "That's terrible!" Then,

frowning, he said, "Or is it? I sort of lost track. Do we still have The Button?"

"It's in my pocket," Mike replied.

"Then we have to do something drastic before we get back to the castle and King Hiram has us frisked," Micky said.

"I guess it's my turn to do something drastic," Peter said.

"Brave lad!" Davy said.

"I'm doing it for all humanity," Peter said. "And nothing's too good for humanity—especially the dogs."

"Stout fellow!"

"Just one thing," Peter said. "When all this is over, and the world is safe for the automobile and the airplane and the electric toothbrush again, I'd like to have a monument erected in my honor. Nothing showy. About the size of the state of Rhode Island would be enough."

"That's the least we could do," Micky said.

"Then I'm ready," Peter said.

"What exactly are you going to do?" Davy asked.

"I'm going to volunteer Mike to swallow The Button," Peter answered.

Mike shook his head. "I couldn't let you do

that," he said. "Suppose someday I ate something heavy and it landed on The Button? The whole civilized world—as we know it—PHROOOOM!"

"Then we'll have to ditch it somewhere along the way and pick it up later, after we finish serving our life sentence," Peter said.

"I like that better than that first drastic idea," Mike said.

"Look. Up ahead." Micky pointed. "See that little table sitting on the sidewalk next to the building? The one with the colorful skirt and the flowerpot on top?"

"The flowerpot with the colorful flowers?" Mike asked.

"Right," Micky replied. "Why not drop The Button in among the flowers? With all that color, who'll notice a black button?"

Mike thought for a moment. "I give up," he answered. "Who?"

"Nobody," Micky replied.

"Say, that gives me an idea," Davy said. "How about dropping The Button in among those colorful flowers in that flowerpot atop that small table with the colorful skirt? Nobody'll notice it there."

Micky shook his head disgustedly. "Of all the dumb ideas. . . ."

"It's our only chance," Mike said. "When we reach that flowerpot, you distract the soldiers' attention some way, and I'll get rid of The Button."

"I just hope, later on, we can remember those flowers," Davy said. "A lifetime is a long stretch."

"We couldn't possibly forget them," Peter said confidently.

"Why not?"

"They're forget-me-nots."

"Hah! You could," Davy replied. "You can't even remember the Alamo."

"What Alamo?" Peter asked.

"Knock it off!" Mike said. "That flowerpot is only a few steps away. Do something!"

As they reached the flowerpot, Micky suddenly halted and pointed up into the sky. "Look!" he cried. "It's a bird! It's a plane! It's—"

"It's none of them!" the leader of the guards growled. "That's that comic book character. He's always flyin' around up there! No more stalling! Get a move on!"

The march continued.

"Did you do it?" Micky asked Mike.

"Yup. It's as safe as a button in a pot full of forget-me-nots."

Davy looked back. "That's only about half-safe," he said. "Remember that little table in the colorful skirt with the flowerpot sitting on it?"

"It rings a bell," Micky answered.

"Well, that little table in a colorful skirt with a flowerpot sitting on it was no little table in a colorful skirt with a flowerpot sitting on it," Davy reported. "It was a lady midget wearing a funny hat."

The others looked back. The lady midget with the funny hat was now strolling along in the other direction. A moment later she disappeared into the crowd.

"Whose turn is it to be the alarmist?" Mike asked.

7

Ring Around the Button

THE SOLDIERS took the Monkees directly to the throne room, where King Hiram, Princess Ellie Jo, and H. P. I. Smith were whiling away the time playing three-handed bridge.

"It's either feast or famine," the king said. "We needed one dummy, and now we have four. Take 'em back to the cell," he commanded the guards.

"One moment, Your Highness," Smith said. "Isn't it possible that these scalawags found The Button? They knew it was in a goose. And they were recaptured in the marketplace. When you put one and one together, what do you get?"

"I don't know. I didn't have to take math," King Hiram replied. "When you're king, the only required subjects are gym and lunch. What do you get?"

"The Button, I hope," Smith replied. "Frisk 'em," he said to the soldiers.

The Monkees were searched. "Nothing, Your Highness," the leader of the soldiers reported.

"They ditched it," Smith guessed.

"Did you?" King Hiram snapped at Peter.

"I cannot tell a lie. George Washington did it," Peter replied.

"Sound the alarm!" King Hiram shouted. "Put out a pick-up for George Washington! I want him brought to me the minute he's found."

Smith leaned across the table and whispered to the king.

"Do tell!" King Hiram said, surprised. "I thought that was Abe Lincoln." He addressed the leader of the soldiers again. "Cancel the alarm." Then to Smith he said, "Do you have any of that truth serum left?"

Smith reached inside his cape and brought out the needle.

"That won't be necessary," Mike said. "We'll

tell you what happened to The Button. It's riding around on top of a lady midget. She's wearing it in her hat."

"Oh, boy!" the king groaned. "The stories get wilder every time. First, it was swallowed by a goose. Now—I won't even repeat it." He signaled to Smith. "Hit 'im with the serum."

Smith got up from the table and cautiously advanced on Mike.

Mike simply rolled up his sleeve. "One way or the other, I'm going to get it," he said. "It might as well be the easy way."

Smith looked disappointed. "I don't work very well the easy way," he said. "It's not natural. Couldn't you resist just a little bit?"

"I'll do it for you," Peter said. "Give me the needle."

Smith held it out to him.

Peter reached for it. "Ouch!" he cried. His eyes became glazed. "I cannot tell a lie," he said. "The Button is riding around on top of a lady midget. Mike dropped it in her hat."

"They did it again!" the king raged. "I never seen such a bunch of lyin' truth-tellers! Lock 'em up!"

The soldiers escorted the Monkees from the

133

throne room and back to the dungeon, where, once again, the guard locked them in the cell.

"I don't know why you boys keep runnin' away," the guard said. "Seems to me this cell ought to be like home to you by now."

"We're proving how normal we are," Davy replied. "It's normal for a boy to run away from home."

"Maybe so," the guard said. "But it sure ain't normal for—"

"Will you just lay off the long hair?" Micky said gruffly.

"I'm only tryin' to be a daddy to you. That's your trouble, I figure. You need a daddy to give you a strong talkin' to. Now, when I was a boy—"

The guard interrupted himself. Princess Ellie Jo, carrying a covered basket, had entered the dungeon.

"Howdy, Princess." The guard beamed. "Can I hold your horse for you again?"

"How thoughtful." Princess Ellie Jo blushed. "Yes, of course you may. It's in the barn."

"I'll get right out there!" the guard said, heading for the door. "It sure is an honor, holdin' a princess's horse."

As soon as the guard was gone, Princess Ellie

Jo handed the basket through the bars to the Monkees.

"Eggs?" Mike speculated.

"Enough to bribe every guard in the palace," she replied.

"Shall we break them now or wait until after she leaves?" Micky asked Mike.

"These eggs you won't break," the princess said. "I hard-boiled them."

Micky, who was holding the basket, lifted the cover and reached in and picked up an egg. He hefted it. "Solid as a rock," he announced. "We couldn't break these if we tried."

"I'll believe that when I don't see it," Mike said. "Let's not take any chances. Put the basket down."

Micky returned the egg to the basket, covered it, then gently placed it on the floor at his feet. "Even if they fell, they wouldn't break—not from that height," he said. "This time, we can't miss."

"So far, not too bad," Mike said. "But what do we do when we get out of here?"

"Paw's already figured that out," Princess Ellie Jo answered. "The circus is playin' in town this week, and he figures that lady midget is part of one of the sideshows. He's gone out to the circus grounds to find her."

"Then there's not a minute to lose," Micky said. "Go get that guard, Princess. We can't bribe him until he gets back."

Blushing, the princess hurried away from the dungeon.

"I'll watch for the guard," Micky said.

He took a step forward to get nearer the bars. As he did, he kicked the basket. It tipped over. Fortunately, thanks to Princess Ellie Jo's forethought, the eggs did not break. But unfortunately, thanks to Princess Ellie Jo's forethought, they rolled from the cell, into the corridor, and out of reach.

"You don't have to watch for the guard anymore," Mike said to Micky.

"I wonder what went wrong," Davy said, frowning. "It seemed like such a sure thing. The princess hard-boiled the eggs. She brought the eggs to us. Micky put them—"

"You passed it," Mike said. "Where it went wrong was when she brought the eggs to us."

Just then, the guard came sauntering back into the dungeon. He had a blissful smile on his face.

"See that," he said, holding out a hand. "That's the hand that held the princess's horse. You know what I'm gonna do with—"

The guard, not watching where he was walking, stepped on an egg. His feet flew into the air. An instant later he landed on the floor with a thud. The blissful smile remained on his face. He was completely unconscious.

"Do you suppose he's some sort of undercover agent and he's really on our side?" Davy mused, studying the guard. "He certainly has been a lot of help to us."

The Monkees reached through the bars, got hold of the guard, and pulled him to the cell. They then relieved him of the key and opened the door. After placing the guard inside the cell on the cot, they locked the door. Then they slipped out of the castle.

"Now, how do we get to the circus grounds?" Mike asked.

"There's Sam on the corner." Peter pointed. "Let's ask him."

They hurried to where Sam Directions was standing. He was reluctant at first, however, to tell them how to get to the circus grounds. He was specializing that day, he advised them, in directions to Battery Park in uptown New York.

"Battery Park is in downtown New York," Mike pointed out.

"Naturally. All my directions are wrong," Sam replied. "It's what people expect when they ask directions from a stranger."

"But you gave us the right directions earlier today," Micky said.

"I was on my lunch hour," Sam explained.

"Well, look. Since we've met before, you're no longer a stranger," Mike said. "So how about giving us the right directions?"

Sam considered for a moment. Then apparently he decided that there was nothing basically unethical about giving the right directions. "Circus grounds, eh?" he said. "Just follow the parade."

After thanking him, they stepped into the street and joined the parade that was passing by, falling in behind the clowns.

The Monkees waved to the people in the crowd lining the street. And the people waved back.

"Look, Mommy!" a little boy cried. "There are the monkeys!"

"Watch how you spell that, kid!" Davy shouted back.

In time, the parade reached the circus grounds and disbanded. The clowns disbanded. The bareback riders and their horses disbanded. The animal wagons disbanded. The elephants disbanded.

And even the band disbanded. Only the Monkees remained together.

"We'd better stay close to the tents, out of sight," Mike said. "King Hiram is probably around here somewhere. And we don't want to go back to that dungeon. Princess Ellie Jo is probably running low on eggs."

"Where will we find the lady midget?" Davy asked.

"In one of the sideshows," Micky said. "Every circus has a midget act. Little people are a big draw."

Leading the way, Mike started around a corner of a tent. But he suddenly drew back.

"King Hiram and H. P. I. Smith!" he whispered. "We almost ran into them. They're right around the corner!"

"I'll bet they've found The Button!" Davy said.

"Then why are they still here?" Micky asked.

"*Shhh!*" Mike said. "Let's try to hear what they're saying."

The Monkees peeked around the corner of the tent. King Hiram and Smith were standing only a few feet away in front of a large advertising sign.

"It just don't make no sense a-tall," King Hiram was saying disgustedly. "Every circus has a midget act. Little people are a big draw. How come this circus don't have no midget act?"

"I don't know," Smith replied, baffled. "All I know is, I've checked every sideshow on the grounds and not one of them is a midget act. I wonder if those boys were really lying when they told the truth."

"Ain't likely," King Hiram replied. "What's more likely is, you saw them midgets and missed 'em. They're itty-bitty, you know. Come on." He motioned. "I'll take a look-see for myself. There ain't nothin' that gets by the king!"

King Hiram and Smith moved off, headed for the sideshow area. As they departed, the sign they had been standing before was revealed. It advertised:

MAIN ATTRACTION!
LADY MIDGET!
Fired From a Catapult!
She Lands on Her Head!

"What do you make of that?" Davy mused.

"It couldn't be important or it wouldn't have got by the king," Peter said.

"Elementary," Mike said. "The king has been

looking in the wrong place. The lady midget isn't in a sideshow. She appears in the main tent."

"Then all we have to do is go to the main tent and find her," Davy said.

"We can't miss," Micky said.

"Unless we're too late," Mike said. "I don't want to be an alarmist, but— Well, I'm a little bothered by that part of her act where she lands on her head."

"If it doesn't bother her, why should it bother you?" Davy asked.

"Do you remember where I put that button?"

"In her hat." Micky nodded.

"And, if she's wearing her hat when she lands on her head, what will she also land on?"

"The Button!" the Monkees cried in unison— and in alarm.

"Stop that act!" Mike shouted, racing toward the main tent, with Micky, Peter, and Davy at his heels.

The Monkees entered the tent and halted. The crowd cheered.

Davy bowed.

"I think they're cheering that elephant that's standing on its nose," Micky said to him.

"I wasn't sure, and I didn't want to take a

chance on offending them if they were cheering me," Davy explained. "You know, an elephant standing on its nose isn't so great. I do the same thing every time I pack."

"You stand on your nose?"

"On my trunk," Davy explained. "I have to, to get it closed. I always pack too much."

"Ladeeees and gentlemen—and children of all ages!" the ringmaster bellowed, standing in the middle of the center ring. "I now direct your attention to the catapult!"

The crowd—and the Monkees—looked toward the far end of the tent. A lady midget, who was wearing a funny hat that looked a lot like a flowerpot, was being lifted up to a catapult.

"Stop! You know not what you do!" Mike called out.

"Look, Mommy! There are the monkeys!" A little boy pointed.

The Monkees strolled over to the box where the youngster and his mother were seated.

"Lady, could you do something about your son's spelling?" Mike begged.

"Yes, he's liable to pull that line sometime when we're right in the middle of a crisis situation," Micky said.

"And if we're distracted," Davy pointed out, "we may fail to resolve that crisis in the nick of time."

"Do you think the cavalry would have ever arrived in time," Peter asked, "if your son had been around shouting, 'Look, Mommy! There's the calvary'?"

"Every fort in the West would have fallen to the savage Indians," Mike said.

"Nonsense!" the woman said huffily. "India is thousands and thousands of miles away."

"Well, now we know where the kid learned to misspell," Mike said to the others. He suddenly scowled. "And, speaking of misspelling, weren't we in the middle of a *cry*-sis situation?"

"May I have your attention!" the ringmaster bellowed crankily. "Ladeeees and gentlemen and children of all ages—the main attraction of the afternoon! Our brave little lady midget will now be catapulted from the catapult! She will travel the entire length of the tent and then land squarely on her head!"

"I knew there was something we had to do," Mike said.

"I think we're too late," Peter said. "We'd better leave it to the calvary."

144

"May I have a drum roll!" the ringmaster shouted.

From the band came a loud drum roll.

"Stop!" Micky cried frantically, rushing up to the bandstand.

"I can't hear you over this drum roll!" the drummer shouted back.

"At the count of ten!" the ringmaster bellowed. "One . . . two. . . ."

The Monkees ran toward the catapult.

"Three . . . four . . . five . . ." the ringmaster counted.

The Monkees reached the catapult.

"Take off your hat!" Mike shouted up to the lady midget.

"Why? Is the flag passing by?" she shouted back.

"Six . . . seven . . . eight. . . ."

"Don't land on your head!" Micky pleaded.

"Ah, you're worried about my brains." The lady midget smiled. "Don't worry, boy. If I had any brains I wouldn't be doing this act."

"Nine . . . ten!" the ringmaster counted.

The catapult fired. The lady midget went sailing high into the air.

"To the other end of the tent!" Mike shouted.

"We'll catch her when she comes down!"

The Monkees dashed back across the three rings. When they reached the far ring, they stopped and, arms outstretched, waited for the lady midget to come down.

"Doesn't she look a little different?" Davy said.

"It's probably because she isn't wearing that funny-looking hat," Peter guessed.

"Her hat!" Mike groaned. "She lost it in midair! It's coming down in the center ring!"

The Monkees raced back to the middle ring. They stood under the hat, waiting for it to reach them.

"Dog take it! There you-all are!" a voice shouted. "And there's that dingdongy hat, too!"

King Hiram and Smith had just entered the tent.

"How'd you find us?" Micky asked. "You're supposed to be checking the sideshows."

"We heard some kid yell, 'Look, Mommy! There are the monkeys,'" Smith replied. "And we took a chance on it being a misspelling."

At that moment, the hat settled into Mike's arms. "Got it!" he cried. "Let's go!"

"Get it!" the king shouted to Smith. "Let's go!"

The Monkees began galloping around the center

ring with King Hiram and H. P. I. Smith in hot pursuit.

"Ladeeeees and gentlemen and children of all ages!" the ringmaster bellowed. "I direct your attention to the middle ring!"

"Could you hold it down a little?" Mike asked the ringmaster as he passed. "This is supposed to be a secret mission we're on."

The lady midget—who had landed on her head in the far ring and had then made her way back to the center ring to find out what all the commotion was about—now got into the act.

"Stop, thief!" she shouted, racing after the king and Smith, who were racing after the Monkees.

"Madame! Are you addressing the king?" Smith asked indignantly.

"I was yellin' at that one in front," she replied. "You was supposed to pass it on."

Smith tapped the king on the shoulder. "Stop, thief! Pass it on," he said.

Obligingly, the king passed the message on. It soon reached Mike, who, by that time, had nearly caught up with the lady midget.

"Stop, thief!" Mike shouted.

The lady midget halted.

Mike tripped over her. Peter fell over Mike.

147

Davy fell over Peter. Micky fell over Davy. King Hiram fell over Micky. Smith fell over King Hiram.

The ringmaster ran around the ring shouting to the crowd. "Don't look! Don't look!" he begged. "Give us another chance!"

"Boo! Boo!" the crowd shouted back.

"Here come the clowns!" the ringmaster announced, signaling frantically. "Everybody watch the clowns!"

A tiny stagecoach pulled by six tiny horses came thundering into the center ring, raising a huge cloud of dust. Clowns began piling out of it. One clown, two clowns, three clowns, four clowns. Each clown was approximately six feet tall— three feet taller than the stagecoach.

A Monkee suddenly appeared from the cloud of dust. It was Mike! Still carrying the hat, he resumed the race around the ring, followed by Peter, followed by Davy, followed by Micky, followed by King Hiram, followed by Smith, followed by the lady midget.

"Say, did you notice anything peculiar about that tiny stagecoach?" Mike said to Peter.

"*Shhh*—I'm counting clowns," Peter replied.

"I'll save you the time," Micky said. "There are fifty-seven of them."

"Thanks," Peter said. Then, addressing Mike, he asked, "Now, what was it you were saying?"

"I asked you if you noticed anything peculiar about that stagecoach."

"You mean that tiny stagecoach that looks like it would hold about three lady midgets, at the out-side, and that fifty-seven six-foot clowns got out of? No . . . what about it?"

"Oh, nothing too exciting," Mike replied. "But it sure raised a big cloud of dust for a little stage-coach like that. I thought that was a little peculiar."

"Maybe it just tries harder," Peter suggested.

"You know, there's one thing that's occurred to me," Davy said. "If that tiny stagecoach holds fifty-seven six-foot clowns, it ought to hold four Monkees, don't you think?"

"I'll try to work that out," Micky said, begin-ning to count on his fingers.

"Even if it doesn't work, it's better than racing around this ring," Mike said. "Next time around —everybody into the stagecoach."

"The king and Smith, too?" Peter asked. "Should I pass it on?"

Mike shook his head. "If we invited them, the lady midget would want to come, too. It'd just be too crowded."

A half-turn later, the Monkees reached the stagecoach. Ducking down, they climbed in. Micky, the last one in, slammed the door.

"Giddyap!" Mike called to the tiny horses.

The horses leaped forward. They galloped from the ring, galloped through the exit, and galloped toward the main highway.

"It's a little cramped in here," Mike commented. "Who's sitting on my neck?"

"That's not your neck—that's my leg," Davy replied.

"Can anybody see where we're going?" Micky asked.

"So far, so good," Peter replied. "We're right behind the horses."

"If I remember my Western movies," Mike said, "somebody ought to be steering."

"There's no steering wheel," Davy reported.

"Look for reins," Micky suggested.

"It's okay. I've got 'em!" Peter said.

"Try again," Mike said. "You've got my shoelaces."

8

Road Block, Monster-Style

THE TINY HORSES—and the stagecoach, with the Monkees inside—reached the main highway, a bumpy dirt road, and kept right on going.

"It might be a good idea to find out where we're going," Mike said. "Does anybody know horse language?"

"Neigh," Davy replied.

"I can laugh in it, but I can't talk in it," Micky said.

"Unfortunately, this is no laughing matter," Mike said. "We have The Button. And we've

151

escaped from King Hiram. But, for all we know, these horses are taking us and The Button right back to the king."

"No. It's okay!" Peter said. "We're headed for the border!"

"How can you be so sure?" Micky asked.

"Elementary," Peter replied. "We know that Bellevue is the shape of a postage stamp. Right? And we know that we were approximately in the center of it. Right? Well, by sighting through the crook of Davy's arm and getting the position of the sun, and comparing it with its position at the exact moment that Sam Directions gave us the right directions—which had to be noon, since he was on his lunch hour—I was able to determine that the horses are traveling north by northeast. And, together with the fact that the castle faces southwest, and the fact that Bellevue sticks up a little at the northwest corner—where it didn't get licked before it was put on the envelope—I was able to calculate the exact speed of the horses. Clear?"

Micky shook his head. "How do you know we're headed for the border?"

"I saw a sign," Peter replied. "It said, 'To the Border.'" He scowled. "Come to think of it, though," he said, "it was pointing in the other direction. Is that important?"

"Probably not," Micky answered. "If we're heading away from one border we must be headed toward the other border."

"There's something else that makes it fairly irrelevant, too," Mike said. He pointed out the rear window of the stagecoach.

Micky and Peter looked. (Davy could not look because he was on the bottom.) They saw that they were being pursued by a large stagecoach pulled by large horses. It was being driven by H. P. I. Smith. And seated beside him was King Hiram.

"I just checked the position of the sun again," Peter said, "and according to my new calculations, big horses run faster than little horses."

"What's going on?" Davy asked from the bottom of the coach. "All I can see is that Mike's elbow is in Micky's eye."

"That's more than I can see," Micky said.

"In about two minutes, you'll be able to see everything," Mike informed Davy. "By then, King Hiram and Smith, who are chasing us in a bigger stagecoach, which is drawn by larger horses, will have caught up with us. And my guess is that after they get The Button they'll pry us out of this

153

cracker box and take us back to the dungeon." He looked thoughtful for a moment. "Unless . . ." he said.

"Unless one of their horses gets a flat hoof?" Peter speculated.

Mike shook his head. "Unless we can find the escape hatch," he said. "Think about it. How is it possible for fifty-seven six-foot clowns to get into a space that's crowded for four normal-size Monkees?"

Peter suddenly brightened. "Of course!" he said.

"How?" Davy asked.

"They looked taller than they were," Peter explained. "They weren't six-foot—they were only five-eleven. Right, Mike?"

"That's possible," Mike replied. "But it wasn't what I had in mind. My guess is that they weren't all in the stagecoach at the same time."

"That's it!" Micky said. "One of them was in Peoria, Illinois. I thought I recognized him. I saw him in Peoria in the spring of '32."

"You weren't even born in the spring of '32," Davy pointed out.

"It must have been somebody else, then," Micky replied. "Sorry to throw a Monkee wrench into your theory," he said to Mike.

154

"That wasn't my theory," Mike said. "My theory is that there's a trapdoor in the bottom of this stagecoach. The trapdoor undoubtedly leads to a tunnel. And the tunnel undoubtedly leads to the clowns' dressing room. Now, see how it's done?"

"I think I understand it," Peter said. "One of the clowns was in Peoria and the others are only five-eleven. Is that it?"

"Close," Mike replied. "Davy," he said, "try to find the trapdoor."

"And hurry!" Micky urged. "King Hiram has practically caught us!"

"I found it!" Davy said excitedly.

"Can you open it?" Mike asked.

"There isn't room—it opens up," Davy replied. "Somebody will have to get out."

"I'll go ride with King Hiram for a while," Peter said. "It looks comfier back there anyway."

"There isn't time," Mike decided. "Micky, you get on Peter's shoulders. That'll give Davy more space."

"I'm already on Peter's shoulders," Micky told him.

"That's not the problem anyway," Davy said to Mike. "It's down here that I need more room, not up there."

155

"Okay, then you crawl up here and get on Micky's shoulders, and I'll open the trapdoor," Mike said.

Davy clambered up Mike, then up Peter, then up Micky, then perched on Micky's shoulders.

"I don't know what you were complaining about," Mike said to Davy. "There's plenty of room down here."

Mike put the midget's hat on the seat of the stagecoach. Then, with both hands, he got hold of the iron ring on the trapdoor and pulled. It opened! Below, he could see a well-lighted tunnel.

"The theory checks out!" Mike reported to the others.

"I knew I saw that guy in Peoria!" Micky said, vindicated.

One by one, the Monkees dropped through the trapdoor into the tunnel. They closed the door behind them and then looked around. The tunnel had been carved out of solid rock. Here and there along the walls there were burning torches.

"It looks like a lake in the Middle West," Peter said.

"A lake?" Micky asked.

"Erie." Peter shuddered.

"Let's get a move on," Mike said. "King Hiram

has probably already caught up with the stage-coach. It won't take him long to find that trap-door. Then he'll be hot on our heels again."

Hurrying, the Monkees proceeded through the tunnel. Then suddenly they came to a fork.

"I don't want to be an alarmist—" Mike began.

"To the left, to the left," Peter urged.

"Now, just a minute," Mike said. "One of these forks goes to the clowns' dressing room and the other goes to the Unknown. Why are you so sure we should go left?"

"I learned that long ago when I was a little kid," Peter replied. "When I was learning to set the table, my mommy always said, 'The knife on the right and—' "

"All right, all right—the fork on the left." Mike nodded.

Taking the fork to the left, the Monkees hurried forward. A few minutes later, however, they were stopped by a wide underground river that was swarming with crocodiles.

"To the left, eh?" Mike said to Peter.

"What do you expect when you take advice from a little kid who doesn't know his left from his right?" Peter replied defensively.

"We'd better go back," Micky said.

"We can't go back," Mike insisted. "King Hiram is in the tunnel by now. If we go back, we'll run straight into him."

"But we can't cross the river," Micky argued. "Those crocodiles look as hungry as alligators."

"I think we can do it," Mike said. "We'll form a human bridge."

"Now, why didn't I think of that," Micky said, disgusted with himself. "All I could think of was to form the Golden Gate Bridge."

"I won't be any help," Peter said. "I cannot tell a lie—I'm the George Washington Bridge."

"You can be in disguise," Mike informed him.

Without further delay, the Monkees formed a human bridge. Micky climbed up on Mike's shoulders. Peter climbed up on Micky's shoulders. Then Davy climbed up to the top.

"Something went wrong," Davy said. "From up here it looks like we formed a human totem pole."

"Patience," Mike said.

Mike moved forward a few steps. He halted at the edge of the river, then leaned forward. The whole totem pole fell. In the nick of time, Davy got a hold on the bank at the far edge of the river. Thus, the Monkees were stretched across the water, forming a human bridge.

"Boy, I bet we'd be something to see at night if we had colored lights," Peter said.

In the distance, a whistle tooted.

"Hurry up!" Davy said. "There's a boat coming and we forgot to be a drawbridge!"

Quickly, Mike crawled up onto Micky's back and then crossed Peter and Davy to safety. Micky followed, crossing over Peter and Davy. Peter was next, crossing Davy. Finally, the other three pulled Davy up onto the bank.

"If a job ever opens up for a bridge, I'm going to have it made," Davy said. "I've had a couple seconds' more experience than the rest of you."

Once more, the Monkees proceeded through the tunnel. They were making pretty good time when all at once, from ahead of them, they heard a terrible roar. They stopped, startled.

"What was that?" Davy asked.

"Well, first off, I think we can eliminate mice, chipmunks, and pussycats as possibilities," Mike replied.

"I think I recognized it," Micky said. "It's the landlord."

"Couldn't be," Peter said. "This isn't Wednesday."

"It came from around that bend in the tunnel,"

Mike said. "The logical thing would be to take a look."

"Right," Micky said. "Let's wait till it peeks around the corner and takes a look at us."

"You know," Davy said, "maybe we were wrong to eliminate the mouse so quickly. It might be a mouse with a bull horn."

"Sure. What are we afraid of?" Micky said. "Mike, you go look."

"Somebody has to do it," Mike agreed. "But I don't want to hog all the glory myself. If one of you—"

In unison, Davy, Micky, and Peter shoved Mike toward the corner.

Mike peeked, looked for a moment, then returned to where the others were waiting. "It's a prehistoric monster," he reported.

"Rats!" Peter said. "I was sure it was going to be a bull with a saxophone."

"Could you be a little more specific?" Micky asked. "There're oodles and oodles of prehistoric monsters. There's the Tyrannosaurus and the Stegosaurus and the Diplodocus and the Ankylosaurus and the Triceratops and the Struthiomimus and—"

"And the Bibliophile," Davy said.

"And the Metatarsal," Peter added.

"I'll describe it," Mike offered. "It's about two stories high—"

"Which two stories?" Micky asked. "Try to be as specific as possible."

" 'Paul Bunyan at Yale' and 'Edgar Allan Poe and His Electric Sister-in-law,' " Mike replied.

"Hey, that's big!" Micky said. "Those are pretty tall stories. Pray continue."

"Well," Mike continued, "it has a body like a two-story rhinoceros, a tail like a mouse with a bull horn at the wrong end, a head like a scoop shovel, and three horns—count 'em—three."

"Yes, yes, keep going," Micky said.

"About eight billion years ago it was a vegetarian," Mike said.

"A triceratops!" Micky, Peter, and Davy cried fearfully in unison.

At that very moment, the terrible roar was heard once again.

"It's coming this way!" Peter shrieked.

"What're we worried about? We're not vegetables," Mike said. "A vegetarian wouldn't touch us with a ten-foot fork."

"But if it's coming this way it'll pass right over us," Micky said.

"That'll make us vegetables," Mike said. "Squash."

The triceratops appeared from around the bend in the tunnel. It halted and stared blankly at them.

"If we can just keep it from moving," Mike said, "maybe we can crawl underneath it and get by it. But if it moves . . . and one of us gets caught under one of those clunky feet. . . ."

"He'll play flat the rest of his life," Micky said, completing the thought.

"That's it!" Mike said. "What is it that soothes the savage beast? Music! We'll play him a tune. And, as soon as he's soothed, we'll crawl past him."

"He doesn't look like much of a music lover to me," Davy said doubtfully.

"Also, we left our instruments back at the castle," Micky said.

"Where's your good ol' American know-how?" Mike challenged. "We'll fake it."

So, faking it, Mike and Peter took up guitars, Micky sat down at the clavichord, and Davy snatched up the tambourine, and they swung into a medley of their favorite songs.

After the first four bars, the triceratops let out another terrible roar. Its giant tail stiffened like a stick.

"We're getting to it," Mike said.

After eight bars the triceratops tried to stuff its feet into its ears.

"He must be turned on," Davy said, "because he sure looks like he's trying to turn himself off."

The triceratops roared once more—this time in total panic. It began retreating. It disappeared around the bend. A moment later the ground began to tremble as the huge prehistoric animal made its escape, lumbering, fear-stricken, into the depths of the tunnel.

"Boy, we sure soothed the pants off that kid," Micky said proudly.

"I don't want to boast," Davy said, "but I think it was my tambourine work that did it. It was the first ring-a-ding-a-ding that put the starch in its tail."

"I just hope all that snorting and roaring didn't stir up the natives," Mike said.

"What natives?" Micky asked.

Mike pointed. A band of savage-looking prehistoric cavemen had appeared around the bend of the tunnel and were peering wildly at the Monkees.

"They don't look stirred up," Davy said. "They look rather friendly." He waved to the cavemen.

"Hello, chaps! Just passing through on our way to the clowns' dressing room."

Beginning to look decidedly unfriendly, the cavemen surrounded the Monkees.

"Mwaga kooka-racha!" the leader said, pinching Davy's arm.

"And they laughed at me in junior high when I took caveman instead of French," Micky said. "If they could only see me now! Boy, they'd still be laughing."

"You mean you understand that language?" Mike asked.

"Speak it like a native," Micky replied.

"What did that one say when he pinched my arm?" Davy inquired.

"He said, 'Season with cloves and bake in a slow oven, twenty minutes per pound.' "

Another caveman spoke up. "Boola-boola hoola hoop!" he said.

"Translation?" Mike said to Micky.

"He's telling the other one we're gods of some kind," Micky replied.

"We're saved!" Davy cried happily.

Micky shook his head. "He was only pointing out that gods take longer in the oven. He was suggesting twenty-five minutes per pound."

"I don't want you guys to think I'm trying to run things," Mike said, "but I think we'd better get out of here."

"Mango-mango, tak to too tango!" the leader of the cavemen said angrily.

"Something about bad manners," Micky translated. "They don't want us to run before they eat."

"Running won't do it anyway," Mike said. "Our best bet is to walk away from here very, very calmly."

"Won't they try to stop us?" Micky asked.

"Not if we play it smart," Mike replied. "Everybody comb your hair over your eyes."

"Scooba-dooba!" the leader of the cavemen objected.

"When he said 'everybody,' he just meant us," Micky explained to him.

Quickly the Monkees combed their hair over their faces. Then nonchalantly they moved through the surrounding cavemen and walked away. Baffled, the cavemen stood rooted. Because, of course, with their hair combed over their faces, the Monkees looked the same from both the front and the rear, and the simple cavemen were unable to tell whether they were coming or going.

When the Monkees reached safety around the bend, they cleared their vision.

"We'll have to try that again next Wednesday when the landlord comes around," Peter said. "Although, frankly, it was a little scary being in there in the dark all alone."

The Monkees continued on their way along the tunnel. Soon they came to a wall of fire. But fortunately there was a door in it, so they passed through it without any trouble.

A while later they came upon a giant who was chanting, "Fee-fie-foh-fum! I smell the blood of an Englishman!"

"That's probably me," Davy replied. "I've had this blood so long it's getting gamy."

The giant was delighted. He had finally found the source of the odd odor that had been bothering him so long. In gratitude, he allowed the Monkees to pass—after getting an assurance from Davy that they would not return.

Not long after that, the Monkees reached a plain, ordinary door, over which, in neon letters, were the words:

CLOWNS' DRESSING ROOM

Mike opened the door, and he and the others dashed from the tunnel. Then instantly they halted.

The clowns' dressing room was a shambles. Trunks were ripped open. Costumes were flung here and there. Clowns were scattered about the room helter-skelter.

"What happened?" Mike asked, dismayed.

Painfully, one of the clowns dragged himself to his feet. "Where were you guys when that wild triceratops went roaring through here?" he asked.

"I don't think we'd better answer that," Mike replied.

The Monkees hurried from the dressing room, then stopped and looked around. The performance had apparently just ended, for a huge crowd was pouring from the main tent.

"Easy does it," Mike said. "We have to get away from here before we're spotted by that lady midget. She probably wants her hat back."

"Why don't we give it to her?" Davy asked. "We don't need the hat, do we? All we need is The Button."

"Right," Micky said. "Show me a man who'd deprive a lady midget of her hat and I'll show you a man who'd deprive a small table with a skirt on it of its flowerpot."

"You're right," Mike said. "We'll give her the hat back."

Spotting Sam Directions nearby, the Monkees asked him the way to the lady midget's tent. He was only too happy to help them. And finally, after wandering around lost for an hour or so, they found the tent that the lady midget called home.

"We brought your hat back to you," Mike said to her.

The lady midget was overjoyed. "I knew you were good boys—in spite of that hair," she said. "Where's my hat?"

"It's right here in my—" Mike began, holding out a hand.

"It's not there," Micky advised him.

"It has to be there!" Mike insisted. "It was there when we were riding in the stagecoach. I remember it as clear as day. I put it on the seat to open the trapdoor. Then I—" He sighed forlornly. "Then I didn't pick it up again," he concluded.

"Where's my hat?" the lady midget demanded.

"Lady, are you sure you were wearing a hat when you mounted that catapult?" Micky asked. "A lot of people make that mistake, you know. They'll climb up on a catapult, thinking they're wearing a hat, and then, an hour later, when they get to the hat-check girl—"

"I want my hat!" the lady midget raged.

"Can you describe it?" Peter asked.

"You might have gone out this morning with a flowerpot on your head," Davy said. "That happens a lot, too."

The lady midget began throwing things.

The Monkees ran from her tent, ducking the bottles, shoes, and vases that were being pegged at them.

"Let that be a lesson to us," Micky said. "A good deed a day is one too many!"

9

The Royal Double Cross

WHEN THE MONKEES reached the edge of town, they noticed that the barrage from the lady midget had ceased. Quick to take advantage of a situation, they stopped running.

"I think we lost her," Mike said, looking back.

"I'm not surprised," Micky said. "Anybody that small is pretty easy to misplace."

"Shall we send out a search party?" Peter asked the others.

"You'll use anything as an excuse for a party, won't you?" Mike said. "But we don't have time for it now. As you may or may not recall, not only have we lost a lady midget, we have also lost a giant tiddlywink."

"That sounds a little suspicious to me," Micky said. "One loss like that in one day might be a coincidence, but two losses in one day smacks of deliberate theft. My guess is that The Button has been stolen. Let's reconstruct the crime."

"First, we stole The Button from Dr. Von Durfull," Davy said. "Next—"

"Not that crime," Micky broke in. "That was just a boyish prank. I'm talking about the crime where The Button was stolen back from us."

"Oh, *that* crime. Well, we were sitting around the pad having breakfast when there came a knock at the door. I opened it, and we found a mysterious stranger outside. Then there was some other stuff and some other stuff and some other stuff and then King Hiram found the lady midget's hat on the seat of the stagecoach."

"A likely story," Micky sneered. "Now, let's have the truth!"

"All right, I confess," Davy replied. "Peter chopped down the cherry tree."

"Me?" Peter objected.

"Think back," Davy said. "There was the cherry

172

tree. There you were with an ax in your hand. Remember?"

Peter shook his head. "The only thing I can remember clearly is the Alamo," he said. "I'll never forget the Alamo."

"That's it! Of course!" Micky said. "That explains it! The Button is now in the possession of King Hiram and/or Dr. Von Durfull!" He smiled victoriously. "See what happens when you ask the wrong questions? You get the right answers. The system never fails."

"All right," Mike said, "now that we know where The Button is, what do we do?"

"Go back to the castle to get it and get tossed in a cell again," Peter replied.

"We've made that mistake often enough," Mike said. "Let's try something else."

"As I see it," Davy said, "our big problem is that King Hiram is the king. If he were just an ordinary everyday bloke like the rest of us he couldn't keep throwing us in the dungeon, could he? So—although I wouldn't even suggest it under any other circumstances—I propose that we overthrow the king."

"Overthrow?" Peter said doubtfully. "He's kind of big to throw overhand. Can't you think of something a little more underhanded?"

"That's exactly what I'm suggesting to you—a revolution."

"That's underhanded enough," Micky agreed.

"We'll need some help," Mike said. "If we try to do it alone, the revolution is going to end up in the dungeon."

"Then, I suggest further," Davy said, "that we locate the nearest exclusive club frequented by the disgruntled rabble and exhort them to rise up against the usurper and strike him down."

"What he say?" Micky asked Mike.

"He didn't say," Mike replied.

Thus, hoping to start a revolution in Bellevue and overthrow King Hiram, thereby regaining possession of The Button, the Monkees entered the town and made their way to the nearest coffeehouse.

The coffeehouse was crowded with patrons, the bulk of whom were in earnest conversation, discussing such matters as instant versus percolated, homogenized milk versus cream versus evaporated milk, and one lump or two.

"This looks like the place," Davy said. "I'd better check, though."

Davy stopped at a table and addressed a young man with an old beard. "Does this place serve as an exclusive club for disgruntled rabble?" he asked.

"A little," the young man replied. "Mostly just coffee, though."

Davy reported to the other Monkees. "With a bit of developing, this can be the place," he advised them.

"What they need is a little pep talk," Micky said, becoming enthusiastic. He strode to a small platform at the far end of the coffeehouse, mounted it, and then faced the patrons.

"All right, you rabbits!" he called.

"*Psssst!* Rabble!" Davy corrected.

"Now hear this!" Micky exhorted, getting the attention of the customers. "Down with antidisestablishmentarianism!"

A great cheer rose from the rabble.

"Say something about the revolution," Davy suggested.

"I just wanted to get them in the mood," Micky replied. Again, he addressed the patrons. "It has come to my attention," he said, "that within days, hours, or possibly even minutes, Bellevue will become the most powerful nation on earth. Now, on the surface, that doesn't seem very serious. I mean, some nation has to be the most powerful on earth—why not Bellevue? But, I ask you: Do we want it to happen here?"

A young man in the audience raised his hand.

"Yes?" Micky asked.

"I want another cup of coffee," the young man replied.

"Very well put!" Micky said. "Fellow rabble," he continued, speaking to all the patrons again, "the question of cost has been raised. Can Bellevue afford to become the most powerful nation on earth? The starving poor all over the world will come begging to our doorstep for eggs! We work hard to lay our eggs! Do we want them to end up in the hands of strangers?"

The audience yawned.

"I think you're losing them," Mike said.

"Down with antidisestablishmentarianism!" Micky shouted.

Alert again, the audience cheered loudly.

"Turn Bellevue into the most powerful nation on earth and we'll be blamed for anything and everything that happens anywhere!" Micky went on. "When the phones are out of order in Alleppey, India, who'll get the blame for it? Bellevue, that's who! Thousands of irate Indians will storm our consulate and burn it to the ground!"

"We'll get the calvary after them," a young man said, bored.

"The revolution. Mention the revolution," Davy urged.

"Perhaps some of you are wondering why I am here," Micky continued. "You're probably asking yourselves, 'What is a brave, handsome, intelligent young man like that doing here in the safety of this exclusive club for the disgruntled rabble, when he should be out leading—or at the very least partici- pating in—the revolt against King Hiram?' Well, it's a good question. And, since you've brought it up, I think I have the right to ask the same ques- tion of you! So—how about it?"

A young lady rose to her feet. "Sugah, what's that ol' cutey-pie King Hiram evah done to us?" she asked.

"What has he ever done?" Micky responded, aghast. "Why from the very first, King Hiram has advocated antidisestablishmentarianism!"

A great roar of anger rose from the crowd.

"Down with the tyrant!" a young man shouted, smashing his coffee cup against a young lady he mistook for a fireplace.

"Up with the revolution!" Micky exhorted.

"Down with mistaking certain people for fireplaces!" a young lady cried.

"On to the castle!" Micky exhorted.

With the Monkees leading the way, the disgruntled rabble surged from the coffeehouse and marched, yelling slogans and tipping over trash cans, toward the castle.

"Isn't this getting a little out-of-hand?" Mike asked. "I had in mind something less violent. I thought maybe we could just make a phone call."

"King Hiram brought this on himself," Micky replied.

"What'd he do?" Davy asked.

"He kept his subjects from having phones."

"That's right. It is all his fault, come to think of it," Davy acknowledged.

As the raging crowd neared the castle, soldiers suddenly appeared at the gate. They raised their rifles.

"Halt—in the name of the king!" the leader of the soldiers shouted.

"Down with the hired assassins!" Micky exhorted the disgruntled rabble.

The rabble, however, had stopped, subdued.

"Storm the gate!" Micky urged.

"I don't know," a young man said. "I don't mind smashing my coffee cup against a young lady I mistake for a fireplace, but goin' up against guys with guns, that's something different."

"This is a revolution," Micky said. "There's bound to be some risk."

"I knew it was gonna be a little risky for the king," the young man replied. "But I didn't have any idea that any of *us* might get hurt. You didn't mention that."

"How about this?" a young lady said. "Why don't we just go back and break up the coffeehouse? It'd be a lot safer."

"Down with the coffeehouse!" a young man shouted.

A cheer rose from the rabble.

"But . . . but . . . but!" Micky objected.

His protest was drowned out by the roar of the crowd as the rabble turned and made its way back toward the coffeehouse, shouting slogans and tipping over more trash cans as it surged through the streets.

"Well, that proves it," Mike said. "You can lead a rabble to the castle, but you can't get it past the gate without a ticket."

"But . . . but . . . but . . ." Micky said, "that's

180

what I was trying to tell them. I have the tickets!"

"All right, why don't we use them ourselves?" Mike said. "We wanted to get into the castle anyway."

The Monkees approached the soldiers, and Micky held out the tickets. "Four on the center aisle," he said. "I hope the curtain hasn't gone up."

" 'Fraid it has," the leader of the soldiers replied, accepting the tickets.

"Down with the curtain!" Davy shouted.

"Ho! You were with that rabble!" the soldier said. He turned his gun on the Monkees. "Hands up, now! King Hiram'll want to talk to you!"

"Is he still king?" Micky asked, surprised. "I heard there was a revolution."

"It got away," Davy said. He pointed in the direction the rabble had gone. "There it goes now!" he said.

"Where? Where?" the leader of the soldiers asked, looking around frantically.

"Follow that finger!" Davy said.

The leader of the soldiers started off, running down the street.

At the same time, the Monkees ran in the opposite direction, toward the castle.

"Seize 'em!" the leader shouted to the other

soldiers, halting and whipping about, having suddenly realized that he was the victim of a clever ploy.

Shots rang out!

The Monkees dashed into the castle.

The soldiers raced after them.

The Monkees galloped up one corridor and down two corridors. Again, shots rang out. The soldiers were only paces behind them.

"That rabble was right, this could be dangerous," Mike said. "Let's find some place to hide until the thing blows over."

"In there!" Davy said, pointing.

Following Davy's finger, the Monkees rushed through a doorway. They slammed the door behind them. They found themselves in a large room that housed a great number of exhibits.

"Anybody know where we are?" Mike asked.

"It said ROYAL MUSEUM over the doorway," Davy replied.

"That's it!" Micky said, inspecting one of the exhibits. "Here's King Hiram's baby shoes, all bronzed and everything."

"Boy, they sure are big," Peter said, amazed.

"They've grown," Micky explained. "It's been a long time since King Hiram was a baby."

182

"Look over here," Davy called from another section of the museum. "Here's the envelope Bellevue was stuck to before it became independent."

"Look at this!" Mike said. "Here's Princess Ellie Jo's sandbox when she was a little girl."

Davy, Micky, and Peter rushed over to see the sandbox.

"Look at all that sand!" Davy said, impressed. "It's almost as big as a desert!"

Peter clutched his throat. "Water! Water!"

Davy wiped his brow. "That devilish sun! I can't stand it!" he sobbed.

"I can't go on!" Micky panted. "Water! Will we never reach the oasis? Are we destined to perish in this wasteland? Water!"

Mike handed him a pistol.

"What's this for?" Micky asked.

"You get a choice," Mike replied. "You can end it all or quench your thirst. It's a water pistol."

"Why must there always be these decisions, decisions, decisions!" Micky wept.

At that instant the door burst open and the pursuing soldiers rushed into the room.

The Monkees jumped behind the sandbox.

"Seize 'em!" the leader of the soldiers shouted.

"Not so fast!" Micky cried. He sprayed the

soldiers with a half dozen rounds from the water pistol.

Two soldiers fell, soaked to the skin, and the others scattered and ducked behind the various exhibits.

"I'll make a deal with you!" the leader of the soldiers called out from behind King Hiram's bronzed baby shoes. "Come out with your hands up!"

"You forgot to mention the rest of the deal," Mike replied.

"I didn't forget," the leader of the soldiers said. "If I told you the rest of the deal, you wouldn't be interested."

"Water!" Peter gasped.

"We're saving it for the pistol," Micky replied.

"I'm getting delirious!" Davy said, staring vacantly across the sand. "I see a mirage!"

Micky squinted into the sun. "I see it, too," he said. "That's a '27 Ford parked in it, isn't it?"

"Mirage not garage," Davy said.

"Same thing," Micky replied. "There wouldn't be a garage out in the middle of a sandbox, so it must be a mirage."

"I'll make you another deal!" the leader of the soldiers called.

"We're not interested!" Micky replied. "We'll die before we surrender!"

"I don't care about you," the leader of the soldiers said. "I've got my eye on that '27 Ford you've got over there in that mirage. What're you asking?"

"The heat's getting him," Micky said to the other Monkees. "Maybe we can disguise ourselves as camels and slip through his lines."

"I say let's jump in that Ford and give 'er the gun!" Davy said.

"Psssst!" a voice behind them hissed.

"What was that?" Peter said, startled.

"That was a *psssst!*" Mike replied. "Don't pay any attention to it. This sand is crawling with them."

"Psssst!" the voice hissed again.

Whipping around, Micky aimed the pistol in the direction of the sound. But he did not fire. He noticed that a secret panel had opened in the wall.

"Psssst!" the voice hissed once more.

"Guys, what sound does a secret panel make?" Micky asked.

The others turned and stared at the opening.

From the darkness came a voice. "Dumplin's, ain't none of you-all gonna come when I say *psssst?*" it asked.

185

"It's the egg lady!" Micky cried happily.

The Monkees dashed from their hiding place behind the sandbox. They raced through the opening. The secret panel closed behind them. Suddenly they were in total darkness.

"We sure want to thank you for coming to our rescue, Princess," Mike said. "How'd you find us out there in that vast wasteland?"

"Never mind that now, dumplin'," the princess replied. "What's important is to get you where that ol' button is. You just follow me."

"We can't see you," Micky said. "It's too dark."

"I'll blush up a little light," the princess said.

She led the way up a stairs, and the Monkees trailed after her, guided by her blush.

"Where is The Button?" Mike asked.

"That ol' Dr. Von Durfull's got it again, sugar," the princess answered.

"But not for long," Mike said confidently. "This time, we'll hang on to it. Now, here's the plan," he continued, addressing the other Monkees. "As soon as we get The Button back, we'll take careful pains to avoid all flocks of geese and lady midgets who look like small tables with flowerpots on top."

"And what then?" Davy asked.

"That's the part of the plan that hasn't been worked out yet," Mike replied. "We'll have to play it by ear."

"Say, doesn't this stairway look a little familiar?" Davy said. "The steps are the same as the one that leads to King Hiram's private chamber."

"How could that be?" Micky said. "Would the princess lead us to King Hiram's private chamber, where he might be waiting to seize us and hold us incommunicado until after he completed taking over the world?"

"Gee, I don't know; that's a puzzler," Mike said. "Ask her."

"Princess," Micky asked, "would you lead us to King Hiram's private chamber, where he might be waiting to seize us and hold us incommunicado until after he completed taking over the world?"

The princess laughed gaily. "What a question!" she said. "Think about it. Would I lead you to the king's private chamber, where he might be waiting to seize you and hold you incommuni-whatsis until after he completed taking over the world?"

"What'd she say?" Mike asked Micky.

"It wasn't what she said, it was the way she said it," Micky replied. "I don't think she understood the question."

"Ask her again," Mike suggested.

"Princess—" Micky began.

"Look! Up ahead! Light!" Davy broke in.

"It looks like a hole in a door," Peter said.

"And familiar, too," Davy said. "In fact, it looks exactly like the hole we busted in the door to the king's private chamber when we broke out of that other secret passageway!"

"Couldn't be," Micky said. "We entered this secret passageway from the museum. The entrance to that other secret passageway was in the library."

"I've got it!" Peter said.

"What?" the other Monkees asked in unison.

"The entrance through which we entered this secret passageway this time wasn't an entrance. It was an exit," Peter replied.

"That's it!" Micky said, alarmed. "I think we've been—"

"Double-crossed!" a voice finished for him.

The door with the hole in it had opened. And standing before them was King Hiram. And beside him was H. P. I. Smith.

Micky turned to Mike. "Do you suppose the princess was hedging when she declined to give me a straight answer to whether she was leading us to the king's private chamber, where he might be waiting to seize us and hold us incommunicado until after he completed taking over the world?" he asked.

"After all she's done for us?" Mike replied. "You sure are a fair-weather believer."

"In!" King Hiram commanded, stepping back and motioning the Monkees through the door into his private chamber.

"I don't care; I'm going to get this settled for once and all," Micky said. He faced the princess. "The truth, now," he said. "Were you hedging?"

"A princess don't hedge, dumplin'," she replied. "Paw had it right. I was out an' out double-crossin' you boys."

"Boy, that's a relief." Micky sighed. "I don't think I could ever trust you again if I found out you were hedging."

"Would it be too much to ask if I asked you why you double-crossed us?" Mike said to Princess Ellie Jo.

"Well, first, 'cause you're born losers," she replied. "And any ol' fool knows that losers don't win ball games."

"I know that." King Hiram nodded.

"And, second," the princess continued, "you-all know what I told you about how terrible it was gonna be when Paw took over the world and everybody on earth had nothin', the same as us in Bellevue, and nothin' wouldn't be worth a hoot nor a holler in a rain barrel after that, status-wise? Well, Paw's done promised me that, after the take-over, me bein' a princess, I'll be entitled to every-thing instead of nothin'. Just so I'll stand out and won't be mistook for some common, ordinary, everyday, run-of-the-mill person."

"Everything?" Micky said dubiously.

"Everything," the princess repeated. "I'll have me an automobile for every day of the week, and an electric toothbrush for every tooth."

"Just carryin' on tradition," King Hiram said fondly. "I gave her a sandbox when she was a little kid."

"I'm even gonna have a telephone," Princess Ellie Jo said. "I reckon you can guess what style it'll be."

Micky got out the water pistol. "Men," he said, addressing the other Monkees, "we have failed in our mission. Now there is only one honorable thing left for us to do."

"I'm ready," Mike said.

"This is a far, far wetter thing we do than we have ever done before," Davy said bravely.

"Could you hold it up a couple minutes?" Peter asked. "I'm not quite ready."

Micky smiled hopefully. "You have some alternative in mind?"

"No; you can get on with the shooting in a minute or so," Peter replied. "I just need some time to locate a dictionary and look up the word 'incommunicado.' "

"Try the library," Mike suggested.

"Right through the secret passageway." Micky pointed.

Peter headed for the opening.

"Halt, you-all!" King Hiram commanded.

"Right. What's your hurry?" Mike said to Peter. "Don't go without us." He turned to King Hiram to explain. "He can't be trusted alone in a library," he said, indicating Peter. "If we're not with him to keep an eye on him he always cuts a finger on page six forty-eight."

"That's the page that has the definition for 'knife,' " Micky said.

Davy, Micky, and Mike followed Peter toward the opening.

"Halt! Halt! Halt! Halt!" King Hiram shouted.

Ignoring the command, the Monkees dashed into the passageway.

They collided with the soldiers who, having found the secret panel, had arrived from the museum.

The Monkees bounced off the soldiers, stumbled back through the opening, quickly regained their balance, turned, and raced to the doorway that led to the corridor. Mike, in the lead, whipped open the door. The Monkees charged through the opening. They collided with the guards the king had stationed in the corridor, bounced off, stumbled back through the opening, failed to regain their balance, and collapsed in a heap at the king's feet.

"We'll make a deal with you," Mike said, looking up.

"Unconditional surrender; that's all I'll accept," King Hiram growled.

"That's what you get when you make snap decisions," Mike said. "If you'd dickered a little, you could have had yourself a '27 Ford."

"Yeah . . . and a mirage to keep it in," Peter added.

10

Out There in Radioland

THE MONKEES UNSCRAMBLED themselves and got to their feet.

"If somebody will just point the way to the dungeon . . ." Mike said.

King Hiram shook his head. "You boys ain't goin' back to that dungeon," he said. "It ain't safe down there."

"Gee, that's thoughtful of you," Peter said. "You're a nice king."

"Ain't safe for me, I mean," King Hiram explained. "You keep escapin'. And the zero hour is comin' up, so I ain't takin' no more chances."

"Within minutes," Smith said to the Monkees, "King Hiram will take over control of the whole world. As you can see, his private chamber has been converted to a broadcasting studio. He will soon make the announcement over the radio."

The Monkees looked around. There was now a large window in one wall of the room. Behind it, a number of engineers were seated at a control panel. In the center of the room was a gigantic boom, and attached to it was a microphone.

"It does look a little different," Micky admitted. He pointed. "Wasn't there a book on that table before?"

"A dictionary," King Hiram replied. "I had it removed; it was a dangerous weapon." He held up a finger, displaying a bandage.

"What's holding up the show?" Mike asked.

"That ol' scientist," Princess Ellie Jo said peevishly. "I just never seen such a dawdler in all my born days!"

Smith nodded toward a third door. "Dr. Von Durfull has The Button in the antechamber," he said.

"Not no more," King Hiram said.

"He's gone?" Smith responded, surprised.

"He ain't gone. But that ain't the antechamber no more," the king said. "It's the anteradio studio." He turned to the Monkees. "He's in there takin' The Button apart to find out what makes it tick," he said.

"Maybe there's a watch in it," Peter suggested.

"We'll soon know," Smith said. "Dr. Von Durfull will be finished very shortly."

"What does he care how it works as long as it does work?" Mike asked.

Smith looked uncomfortable. "It wouldn't matter to us," he said. "But some of the heads of state of the other countries insist on knowing."

"Soreheads!" King Hiram grumbled.

"You see, as a courtesy, we sent out notices of the take-over to the heads of state," Smith explained. "But, instead of going along, as any well-mannered head of state would do, some of them voiced some doubts about The Button."

"They said, 'How do we know it'll work?' " King Hiram muttered. "Talk about nerve!"

"You should have just punched it and blown them up," Davy said. "It would have served them right."

"We were in kind of a bind on that," Smith said. "If we'd blown them up, there wouldn't have been any world left to take over, would there?"

"And I would've lost my sponsor," King Hiram said.

Mike blinked at him. "Your announcement of the take-over of the world is sponsored?" he asked.

"Big outfit that makes world globes," King Hiram replied. "It's a natural tie-in."

Smith looked at his watch. "What's keeping Von Durfull?" he said anxiously. "We're coming up on air time."

"What exactly is Dr. Von Durfull doing?" Mike asked.

"He's takin' that ol' button apart part by part," Princess Ellie Jo replied. "Thataway, he's gonna find out what makes it work. Then Paw can tell it to all them doubtin' Thomases."

"I'm feelin' a little sick-sick in my tum-tum," King Hiram complained.

"Stage fright," Smith diagnosed. "You'd better lie down."

King Hiram went to the bed and stretched out.

Princess Ellie Jo departed to get her father some seltzer.

At that moment, the sponsor appeared in the engineer's booth, and Smith went to talk to him.

The Monkees were left alone.

"Anybody have any ideas?" Mike asked.

"I think we ought to try to get a couple minutes on King Hiram's program," Peter said. "The whole world will be listening. We could use that kind of exposure."

"I was thinking more about an idea to get The Button back," Mike said.

"We could rush the anteradio studio, overpower Dr. Von Durfull, retrieve The Button, then flee," Micky said.

"There are guards at one door and soldiers at the other," Davy pointed out.

"We could jump out an anteradio studio window," Micky said.

"We're three stories up," Mike said.

"Then it'll take a little longer," Micky said. "First, we'll have to get the bulldozers in and remove the first two stories, dropping the third story to the ground floor. Then—"

"We'd never make it," Mike said. "It's almost air time."

"How's this?" Peter suggested. "While King Hiram is on the air, I'll stand behind him shaking my head. Then the audience will think it's all a hoax. And if nobody pays any attention to the announcement, life will go on as it always has before."

"Great—except for one minor thing," Micky said. "This is radio, not television. The audience wouldn't see you."

"Not even if they got up close to their sets?"

"We might as well face it," Mike said gloomily. "We're licked."

At that moment, H. P. I. Smith returned from the engineer's booth. He was accompanied by the sponsor, a large, potbellied, balding man who was puffing on a long black cigar. Smith introduced him to the Monkees.

"Congratulations," Mike said to the sponsor. "It looks like you've got a hit on your hands."

"I don't know," the sponsor said worriedly. "It's a little risky, sponsorwise. Taking over the entire world. . . . It's never been done before. I'm worried about how the audience will react. I'm gonna get letters, I'm sure of it."

"If you get letters, you just let King Hiram know about it," Smith said. "He'll have the letter writers tossed in the dungeon."

"That don't sell world globes," the sponsor grumbled.

"Here's an idea," Mike said. "Instead of putting the program on the air, why don't you film it and then keep it in storage for a couple years? In time, you could bring it out as an old movie."

"Say. . ." the sponsor replied, brightening.

"King Hiram would never accept that," Smith said.

The sponsor clouded over again. "Stars!" he muttered. "They can never see the businessman's point of view."

Princess Ellie Jo came back into the room. She delivered the seltzer to her father and then joined the group that included the Monkees, Smith, and the sponsor.

"I'm the one who needs that tum-tum stuff," the sponsor said. "I've got a lot of eggs riding on this show."

"You look troubled, dumplin'," the princess said sympathetically. "How's that? You're gonna get the highest Nielsen in the whole history of show business."

"Hah! But how'll it go down imagewise? That's the question," the sponsor said. "A take-over is always controversial. I just wish the space program was further along. I'd like to try this show out on Mars before it plays Earth."

King Hiram sat up. "What's keeping that clod with The Button?" he complained.

"I'll check on him, Your Highness," Smith said.

He went to the door of the anteradio studio and knocked. There was no response. He knocked again. Again, there was no reply. Smith put an ear to the door.

"What's going on!" King Hiram roared.

"I think I hear weeping," Smith reported. He opened the door and looked in. "I heard weeping," he said.

Smith disappeared into the anteradio studio.

The king jumped up and followed him.

The Monkees and the sponsor tagged after them.

They found Dr. Von Durfull seated at a work-table, his face buried in his arms, sobbing. Spread out on the table were a great number of small parts.

"Stop that!" King Hiram raged. "If there's anything I can't stand, it's a cry-baby scientist!"

Dr. Von Durfull raised his head. He dried his tears.

"How's it goin'?" King Hiram asked cautiously.

"I'll give you a hint," Dr. Von Durfull replied. "After today, you can go back to calling me Dr. Von Schnook."

"You mean you haven't figured out yet how it works?" Smith said.

"I can give you a general idea how it used to work," Von Schnook replied.

"How?"

"You pushed down on the top."

"Excuse me for insinuating myself into a situation that's basically not really any of my concern," Mike said to Dr. Von Schnook. "But did you say 'used to' work?"

"That was a slip of the tongue," Smith said hopefully.

"It was a slip of the fingers," Dr. Von Schnook corrected him. "I got The Button apart, but I can't get it back together. Good-bye, Button."

"Outrage!" the sponsor roared. "I paid good eggs for this show, and it's supposed to include The Button. I've been had! I'll take this to the Supreme Court!"

"I can save you some time," Micky said. "The verdict is 'Guilty.' Where you made your mistake was when you complained about being swindled."

"Hold on!" King Hiram said. "Ain't nobody been swindled—yet. The trouble is, I been dependin' on a dumb-headed overeducated scientist. Them's the kind that don't know nothin'. What this calls for is some good ol' everyday, common, ordinary common sense. Anybody can put a button back together if he don't know what he's doin'!"

"Of course!" Micky agreed. "Some of the greatest inventions of all time have been developed by good ol' everyday, common, ordinary tinkerers. Look at the Wright brothers. They thought they were building the world's biggest window fan."

"And then, all of a sudden, there it was—the paddle-wheel riverboat!" Peter said.

"Quiet!" King Hiram shouted. He picked up a part from the table. "I got to get this dingus put back together before air time."

"Could you use some help?" Micky asked. "I once took a wristwatch apart and put it back together again."

"Perfect?" King Hiram asked warily.

"I'm not sure," Micky replied. "Does Mickey Mouse wear gloves on his ears?"

"I'll lend a hand, too," Mike said. He picked up a part. "This looks like a frabbis," he said, studying it. "If I remember right, a frabbis connects to a blipp."

"To a blipp!" Davy said scornfully. "You attach a frabbis to a blipp and you know what you'll get? You'll get a frippus, that's what you'll get. That's probably the whole problem, as it is; somebody's connected a frabbis to a blipp. Boy, are you guys lucky I'm here!" he said, shoving the others aside and stepping up to the table. "I'm probably the only person in Bellevue who knows better than to— Hey!" he said, beaming. "Look here!" He picked up a part. "Here's the crank to Uncle Harry's electric ice-cream freezer! He's been wondering for years where it had got to!"

"Get out of my way!" King Hiram raged.

Davy chucked the part he had picked up out the nearest window.

"Now, what'd you do that for?" King Hiram exploded.

"Uncle Harry's down there waiting for it," Davy explained.

"Been down there for years," Mike confirmed. "I was talking to him just yesterday. 'Frank,' he said—"

"Why did he call you Frank?" Davy asked, puzzled.

"Isn't that my name?" Mike asked.

"Oh, sure, that's your name," Davy replied. "But I didn't know Uncle Harry knew it."

"Come to think of it, I didn't either." Mike scowled. "You know, I'll bet that wasn't your Uncle Harry I was talking to."

"Was he a short, tall man with a fat, skinny

build and standing on one foot?" Davy asked.

"Which foot?"

"Middle."

"No," Mike replied. "This was a tall, short guy with a purple moustache."

"Aha!" Davy exclaimed. "And it was Monday. Right?"

"You know who it was?"

"Of course! It was Aunt Bessie. She always stands in for Uncle Harry on Mondays."

"Are you two funny talkin' boys finished?" King Hiram inquired. "If you are, will you get away from my table and let me get at them button parts?"

"Clear the way!" Mike shouted.

"That's better," King Hiram said, moving up to the table.

"We'll just tidy up for you so you'll have room to work," Mike said. He picked up a handful of parts and tossed them out another window. "Better?" he asked, smiling.

King Hiram turned, without a word, and clomped wearily from the room.

The others moved to the doorway and looked into the radio studio. King Hiram was stretched out on the bed.

Princess Ellie Jo entered the radio studio from the corridor. She was carrying an ice bag, which she placed on her father's brow.

"I went to get it when I heard that dumb ol' scientist was cryin'," she explained. "I just knew it was gonna turn out this way."

The sponsor stormed over to the bed and shook his fist in King Hiram's face. "I demand my eggs' worth!" he demanded. "You sold me a show. If the show don't go on, I'll have you blacklisted in every radio studio in the world! You'll never practice show biz again!"

"Have pity, fella," King Hiram pleaded. "I've got a head like the Fourth of July. Tell you what I'll do," he said. " 'Stead of that show I promised you, I'll execute them four boys that's the cause of all this trouble. Will that suit you?"

"That don't sell world globes!" the sponsor screamed.

"If getting executed won't help, maybe we could do something else," Mike suggested.

"Shhh!" Micky said. "Don't be too eager. Let's hold out for our top price—the execution."

"This is a crisis," Davy said. "We can get executed anytime. I say we ought to settle for something less. This one time, anyway."

"If we do it once, we'll have to do it again," Micky argued.

"Say, uh, what is it you four boys got in mind?" the sponsor asked.

"Well, you need a show," Mike said. "And, we're kind of entertainers. So, for enough eggs, we might be talked into going on in place of King Hiram and The Button."

"Entertainers like how?" the sponsor asked.

"I play and sing and these other three do an imitation of me playing and singing," Davy told him.

"Hey! That's good!" the sponsor said. "I like imitations." He frowned. "Unless they're controversial," he added.

"Tell you what I'll do, boys," King Hiram said, sitting up and removing the ice bag. "You go on for me and get me out of this spot I'm in with my sponsor, and someday, if you can catch me, I'll do something for you in return."

"You can do something now," Mike said. "You can trot down to the throne room and get our instruments. That's where we left them this morning when you threw us in the dungeon."

"Is that what them was?" the king asked, astounded. "The queen mother thought they was some new kind of pot. She's had 'em on the stove all day."

"Good. We won't have to warm them up before we go on the air," Mike said.

The king hurried off to fetch the Monkees' instruments.

"Ain't this nice!" Princess Ellie Jo said. "Looks like we're gonna have a happy endin' after all."

"Yes, these fine boys, my fellow Americans and that one Britisher, have saved the world from nothin'," H. P. I. Smith said. "I'm proud of them. It's been an honor to have been on their side all along in spite of the way things may have looked at times."

"You didn't fool us for a minute," Davy said.

"I was a little suspicious of him there when he was yelling, 'Seize 'em! Seize 'em!' and chasing us up and down the corridors," Peter said.

"I was imitating the king," Smith said. "That's what he was yelling."

"Sure wish I could have seen that," the sponsor said. "I like imitations."

King Hiram came hurrying back into the studio, carrying the Monkees' instruments.

"Easy," the king cautioned. "The handles are still a little hot."

Armed with their instruments, the Monkees stepped up to the microphone. The "On The Air" sign flashed on.

"Howdy, all you friends and neighbors out there in radioland," Mike said. "First off, I got a little announcement to make. Due to a whole lot of dumb luck, the program originally scheduled for this time will not be heard. The commercials, however, will go on just as planned."

"That's a nice boy!" The sponsor beamed.

"Now, if you'll just move up close to your sets and adjust the color knob," Mike continued, "we'll play you a tune or two."

The Monkees began to sing, and the sponsor's smile grew wider.

"I like it," he glowed. "They sound a lot like that outfit on the TV, eh—the Monkees?"

"They got a smack of sameness to 'em, all right," Smith agreed.

"Only better!" the sponsor declared. "The real thing, anybody can do. But a first-class imitation like that—that's talent!"

Whitman CLASSICS

The Hound of the
    Baskervilles

Tales to Tremble By

More Tales to Tremble By

Seven Great Detective
    Stories

Black Beauty

Tales From Arabian Nights

Little Women

The Call of the Wild

Tom Sawyer

Robin Hood

The Wonderful Wizard
    of Oz

Robinson Crusoe

Wild Animals I Have
    Known

The War of the Worlds

Stand By for Adventure

Huckleberry Finn

Alice in Wonderland

REG. U.S. PAT. OFF.

*Start your home library of
WHITMAN CLASSICS now.*

Whitman ADVENTURE and MYSTERY Books